Emerald DARKNESS

Beautiful Darkness, Book 1

Emerald DARKNESS

Beautiful Darkness, Book 1

SARRA CANNON

Emerald Darkness

Find Sarra Cannon on the web!
www.sarracannon.com

Cover design by Robin Ludwig
Editing Services provided by The Atwater Group

ISBN: 978-1-62421-038-9

Books By Sarra Cannon

Young Adult

Peachville High Demons series:
Beautiful Demons
Inner Demons
Bitter Demons
Shadow Demons
Rival Demons
Demons Forever

A Demon's Wrath Part 1
A Demon's Wrath Part 2
After Midnight

New Adult

Fairhope series:
The Trouble With Goodbye
The Moment We Began
A Season For Hope
The Fear of Letting Go

Sacrifice Me
The Demon: Episode 1
The Dream: Episode 2
The Darkness: Episode 3
The Dying: Episode 4
The Devil: Episode 5
The Doorway: Episode 6

"Deep into that darkness peering,
long I stood there, wondering, fearing,
doubting, dreaming dreams no mortal
ever dared to dream before."
Edgar Allan Poe

.

Only A Dream

Harper

The moon peered through the dark clouds, creating a crisscross pattern of shadows on the forest floor. I darted between them, my feet light and careful, every step a chance to be discovered.

Or followed.

Miles from home, all alone, chasing a truth I didn't even understand. This would be the perfect way to end me.

I adjusted the black hood covering my blonde hair and glanced behind me. I didn't dare to breathe, afraid the sound might cloak a misplaced footstep or snap of a twig. I counted to ten, my eyes searching for any sign of movement.

But nothing moved.

The forest was still and quiet, as if it somehow shared my fear.

What was I doing here? I couldn't shake the feeling that once I got to my destination, nothing would ever be the same again. Something secret had been set in motion and once I discovered it, there would be no going back.

I ducked low, my heart racing. Was she out there this time? Watching me?

In the back of my mind, a part of me realized this was only a dream, but it didn't slow the beating of my heart or calm the butterflies dancing in my stomach.

When I was confident I had not been followed, I moved again, darting toward the next shadow, my blood pumping as the trees thinned to reveal a small circular clearing several feet ahead. I made my way to the edge of the woods and paused to study the small shabby house situated perfectly in the center of the clearing.

This was new.

Most nights, I ran through the woods, fear stalking me like a hunter, never knowing where I was headed or who was behind me. Sometimes, I got a rare glimpse of the woman in black, her dark hood pulled over her head to hide her face.

But I'd never seen a house before.

There were no roads or worn paths leading up to the front door. Brown, brittle grass and weeds had grown up as high as my knees in most places. It looked completely abandoned. No lights shone through the windows. No shadows moved beyond the broken glass.

A simple porch was attached to the front, but it was barely more than a few boards nailed together. Strips of white paint had been removed by the weather over the years, leaving the place looking dull and brown and haunted. There was no front door. Only an empty black hole. A heavy sorrow overwhelmed this place, hanging in the air around it like a thick perfume.

I found myself wishing for Lea. Even in my dream, the thought of her name made my stomach tense. I had hurt her, and it devastated me, but she was part of our group, and I needed her. If she were here, she could reveal the secret tragedies this place had seen. Her gift of conjuring memories might have been useful, but I had a feeling I did not want to know the horrors of this place.

The moon disappeared behind the clouds again, and the clearing slipped into complete darkness.

I should move now, but fear sank down to the pit of my stomach like a heavy stone, anchoring my feet to the ground.

Was it a trap? What would I find inside?

I couldn't shake the feeling of death that hovered near me, breathing down my neck.

My lips parted, and I inhaled a ragged breath. I leaned my forehead against the cool, rough bark of the pine tree and closed my eyes. I pictured the drawing Jackson, my fiancé, had given me shortly after our final battle with Priestess Winter several months ago. A king and queen seated on a soft blanket in a sunny field, hands clasped as they watched their son playing in the grass. A promise of happier days to come.

Jackson's visions always came true. There was no avoiding them.

Usually, that was a bad thing, but this one vision, this one drawing, had given me peace. I clung to it like life.

I touched my palms to the tree and waited for the essence of its power to fill me, feeling its roots snake through the soil under my feet. I became a part of the earth around me, connecting that secret well of strength deep inside my core to the river of energy that pulsed through every living thing.

When my eyes snapped open, my hands disappeared. I became the color of air and nothingness, invisible to the normal human eye. I crouched and slipped into the high grass.

No turning back now.

The boards on the steps leading to the porch groaned under my feet, and I paused, waiting. I watched for movement through the dark windows.

I stepped more carefully, moving with aching slowness as I crossed the threshold into the house. It was somehow colder inside than it was out in the woods, and goose bumps prickled my arms and legs.

I thought of the strange female voice that always spoke to me in my dreams.

Please. Listen. Darkness is coming for you. Find me there, and I will steer you toward the light.

Was she trying to help me? Or was this another in a long line of betrayals?

I reached for the gold locket hanging from a chain around my neck. A gift from Jackson, his heart stone locked inside like a secret meant only for me. It had never been with me in my dreams before, and I drew strength from its presence, praying that whatever darkness we were about to face could be survived, as long as we had each other.

I let my invisibility drop and stood shivering in the small, one-room shack of a house in the middle of the woods.

With a trembling hand, I conjured a small orb of white light and sent it to the center of the room. The house was completely empty, except for one thing. A cage made of black iron, its door wide open.

Hot blood pumped through my veins. I had seen cages like this once before in the dungeons of Winterhaven. Priestess Winter, the leader of the sapphire demon gates, had locked away witches who crossed her or disobeyed her, forcing them to live in iron cages suspended fifty feet in the air while their life and power drained from their bodies.

For her evil, I had killed Priestess Winter with my own bare hands, ripping what served for a heart straight from her chest.

And I knew that someday her sisters would want their revenge for what I had done.

Something very dark and very dangerous was on the horizon, and now I understood what all these dreams had meant. I understood why the cloaked woman had come to me in my sleep, urging me to listen.

My eyes locked on something lying on the floor of the cage.

I stepped forward and lowered my orb inside to get a closer look. My mouth went dry at the sight of it and a cry escaped my throat.

There, on the floor of the cage, was the symbol of my late father's love for my mother—a single, pure white rose. It was a symbol of all that was good inside me. The white roses were our secret portal between worlds, allowing us to pass from the human world of my birth into the Shadow World of my newfound demon heritage.

The sight of it struck me so hard it brought me to my knees against the dusty floor, but it wasn't the flower that had rattled me.

It was the fact that the rose was wrapped in a strand of dark green emeralds.

Sarra Cannon

An Unwelcome Spark

Lea

The witches were barely visible through the trees. Ten of them, more than a hundred yards away. It would be a challenge, but I had never been one to back away from a fight. The harder, the better.

Tell me I couldn't do something, and I would prove you wrong every damn time.

I pushed one foot forward and lifted my bow. I nocked a ghostly arrow and drew back on the string. I aimed at the first witch, taking a deep breath and letting go on the exhale.

I didn't wait to see if my first arrow found its mark. I quickly nocked another conjured arrow and shot again and again, the string making a satisfying thumping sound as each arrow released.

By the time my breath was gone, I had sent all ten arrows toward the conjured witches. I lowered my bow to my side and counted my kills, my heart racing.

Each target had a glimmering arrow through its shadowy heart.

I allowed a hint of a smile to tease my lips, but I had celebrated too quickly.

I'd hit every mark except one. Number six. I trudged through the thick pine straw on the forest floor, kicking at the fallen limbs in my path. My hand clutched the grip of my bow so tightly, I worried I might break yet another one.

Teeth clenched, I studied the sixth conjured witch. The arrow was seated deep in her left arm, which was the useful equivalent of a freaking mile away from her heart.

Nine out of ten was unacceptable. In a real battle, witch number six could have been the death of me or someone I loved.

Right now, if that person was Harper, I might not mind so much. In fact, it didn't escape my notice that half the conjured witches on this round had faces that resembled hers. But anyone else dead as a result of my poor aim would be a tragedy.

With a wave of my hand, the figures dissolved. All traces of my victory smile were gone, replaced by an anger and sorrow I wasn't ready to face. Not yet.

The snap of a limb nearby brought my bow back up, arrow ready, but I lowered it as Aerden walked into a thin strip of moonlight between the trees. He better not have come to lecture me about using my powers out here in the woods. Tomorrow morning, I'd have to beg Zara to regrow some of the trees I had ruined by pulling from their life force in order to cast.

"I almost shot you," I said.

"Normally I would say keep dreaming, but you're getting scary," he said. He motioned toward the area where the targets had stood moments before. "How many this time? Eight?"

"Ten," I said.

He raised an eyebrow, and our eyes met through the shadows. "You're improving quickly."

I shook my head and looked away. "I missed one."

A smile played across his lips and quickly disappeared. "One target out of ten at a hundred-yard distance?" He shook his head and sighed. "Pitiful."

"Don't start with me," I said, heading back toward Brighton Manor. Not tonight. "When the fighting begins again, even one miss could mean the difference between victory and seeing everything we've worked for destroyed."

He grew quiet and stared up at the sky. The moon was barely visible through the tops of the pine trees. Sadness stretched between

8

us, the heaviness of a hundred years behind its strength.

Even though he'd been free for several months now, Aerden wore his despair like a dark cloak draped over the shell of who he used to be. It would disappear for brief moments, but a simple word or expression could bring it back in the blink of an eye.

Mentioning the coming war was a mistake.

I had learned not to bug him about his moodiness, never pushing him to tell us about his years as a demon slave to the Order of Shadows. Talking about it only seemed to make it worse. Besides, his twin brother Jackson bugged him about it enough for all of us.

Around me, I allowed him to be silent. I think that's why he always sought me out when I was alone here in the dark, training. He once told me he'd had voices in his head for so long, silence was the only way he could be sure he was free.

"Not going to try again?" he asked when he caught up with me.

"Why? You want a go at it?" I asked. I had come out here to be alone, but maybe I'd spent enough time sulking in the shadows for one night. Besides, I was glad he had spared me the lecture. Harper didn't like for us to train out here in the open where our destruction could be easily seen and tracked, but considering she'd just gotten engaged to the demon I once loved, I didn't really give a crap.

"I could be persuaded to participate," he said.

I stopped and smiled, glancing back at my makeshift training grounds. "As ally or enemy?"

"Anyone who dares to be your enemy is a fool," he said. "Ally for sure."

I nodded and reset the course, adding ten additional witch targets in a row behind the first ten.

Aerden and I had trained a lot over the past few months. At first, his skills were rusty. He sometimes struggled to shift forms and his confidence was nonexistent after all this time of being forced to do whatever his host witch commanded or needed of him. But his instincts were still there.

Other than shifting from solid form to demon shadow, he never used his powers. He preferred physical weapons, everything from axes to swords to spears.

He'd been a great warrior once. Even better in battle than his twin brother, Jackson. It was good to see him training again.

"Why don't you try magic this round?" I said as casually as I could, barely glancing at him as I walked toward my starting mark.

Even fifty feet away, I could feel him tense.

"Maybe next time," he said, the playful tone gone from his voice. In my peripheral vision, I saw him lift a hand to the spear strapped to his back.

I prepared my first conjured arrow and took a deep breath. With a subtle nod of my head, he shifted to black smoke and flew through the air toward the targets, gracefully dodging my arrows as he rushed toward the witches on the second row. He moved so fast my eyes couldn't keep track of him.

His skill distracted me, and I slowed the release of my arrows just to watch as he shifted back and forth from solid form to shadow, his spear twirling, landing each blow and stab with such precision, it awed me. The targets fell to the ground so quickly that by the time I released my seventh arrow, the target I'd been aiming for was already gone.

Aerden returned to his solid human form just in time to catch the crest of my arrow with his bare hand.

My lips parted, and our eyes met across the distance. Breathless, he watched for my reaction.

An unwelcome spark ignited in my chest.

"Impressed?" he asked, one eyebrow raised, his head cocked slightly to the side. He still held the burning arrow in his hand.

Impressed was not the word I'd been thinking of.

"Not bad," I said, clearing my throat and trying to understand the fluttering feeling in my stomach. I waved my hand in the air and the brutalized targets disintegrated into nothing. "For a guy with a primitive weapon."

"Hey, if I had my axe back, I'd have taken down more of them."

He laughed and tried to hide his smile. Hell, even a hint of a smile from him felt like a victory. I longed for the days of our childhood when we laughed all the time and had no idea of the terrors that awaited.

But that was before our lives were stolen from us. Before our past happiness became the pain we had to bear in silence.

We walked side by side through the forest toward the house, the warmth of that one smile from him soaking into me like sunlight. His arm brushed against mine, and I felt myself wanting to lean into him.

Instead, I moved away.

Sarra Cannon

More Important Things

Lea

Footsteps sounded behind us. Aerden and I both raised our weapons without hesitation.

We were all on edge these days.

A man with black hair smiled and lifted his hands in surrender. "I come in peace," he said, his thick Spanish accent apparent even in his laughter.

"That's the second time I almost shot someone tonight," I said. I secured my bow across my shoulder and reached out to grip his hand. Andros pulled me into a strong hug. "You guys should both know better than to sneak up on me. Especially tonight."

"Why especially tonight?" Andros asked, releasing me and holding his hand out to Aerden. "Has something happened?"

"Her former betrothed got engaged," Aerden said, gripping Andros's hand in welcome.

I shot him a look. I hadn't realized he understood why I was out here training tonight, but Aerden constantly surprised me that way. In the same way that I never asked him about his years as a slave, he never asked me to talk about what really happened between Jackson and me. It was an unspoken agreement between us, but he seemed to understand how much it affected me, even after all this time.

"Engaged?" Andros asked, his eyes darkening. "How can this be? Unless you have given him your permission, Princess?"

"Do you think I could really deny it?" I asked. "He proposed at the Halloween party. Which you bailed on, by the way. I thought you said you were going to bring Ourelia."

I missed spending time with Andros, his wife, Ourelia, and their young daughter, Sasha. We had spent many years together in the Shadow World before I came over to this side, and even though a few of my best friends had come through with me, this world was often a very lonely place. Strange how you could sometimes be surrounded by people and still feel alone.

Especially when you lived with the demon you used to love more than life itself and the new girl he loved more than you.

I definitely did not want to talk about it.

"There will be plenty of time for parties once the Order of Shadows is defeated," Andros said. "For months now, we have been waiting. Doing nothing while the Order continues to kidnap demons from our lands and force them into slavery."

"Thousands of demons free and home with their families," Aerden said. "You can't say we've done nothing."

Andros shook his head. "I do not mean to sound ungrateful for all your group has accomplished," he said. "But freeing the sapphire gates is not enough. For every demon that has been set free from slavery in this world, two more are being kidnapped. The four remaining priestesses of the Order have doubled their recruitment over the past few months. Something must be done."

"Is that why you're here?" I asked. Andros didn't come to the human world very often. He hated it here. He hated humans in general, really, and every time I saw him lately he tried to convince me to take stronger action against the Order. He didn't understand why I was allowing Harper, a young human girl, to give the orders around here.

Hell, sometimes I didn't understand it myself. But Harper was the one who had saved Aerden when all the rest of us had failed. No matter how I felt about her personally, she deserved my loyalty and my trust.

Besides, she was half-demon, a princess in her own right.

"I'm afraid I've come for much more important matters," Andros said, his expression growing dark and tense. He glanced at Aerden. "May I speak freely, Princess?"

"Yes, of course," I said. But just in case, I turned to Aerden and added, "As long as you understand that anything discussed here stays between the three of us."

Aerden questioned me with his eyes, but nodded.

Andros cleared his throat and looked around, as if making sure no one else was listening.

"I try to keep eyes and ears on your father's city in the Northern Kingdom," he said. "But six months ago, after the fall of the sapphire demon gates, your father closed the gates of his own city. No one has been allowed to enter or leave since."

I already knew this, so I waited for him to say more.

"But I do have a few of my men who are still inside. I haven't heard from them in six full months, but a few hours ago, a messenger arrived at the secret entrance to the Underground. He had the tattoo of a phoenix on his arm."

My eyes widened. "My father's insignia."

The Underground was the home of the Resistance Army, a group of hundreds of demons and their families who had banded together, vowing to fight against the Order and protect the demons outside the safety of the King's City. Andros led the army, and when Jackson and I first found out the truth about the Order, about what had happened to Aerden and so many thousands of demons from our world, we had joined the Resistance ourselves for many years.

As far as we knew, neither my father nor his guards knew the location of the Resistance forces.

"How—"

"One of my men inside must have trusted the guard enough to tell him where to find us," Andros said. "That alone should tell you just how important it was that I receive his message."

"What did he say?"

"Lea." The way he said my name sent chills down my spine. Andros was one of the bravest, most stubborn demons I had ever met. He hardly knew the meaning of fear, but there was unease in his voice and in his eyes as he spoke. "He said your father has brought a stone guardian with a diamond heart to Leuxia, the King's City."

My entire body froze, each muscle tense and unmoving. I couldn't breathe. A gentle wind blew across my skin, a loose strand of hair from my braid fluttering against the back of my neck.

I shivered.

"That's not possible."

"I wouldn't have thought so, either," Andros said. "But one of the King's Guard taking such a risk to seek me out? He risked his life coming to me. I could have killed him for his knowledge of the Underground."

"I thought stone guardians were a myth," Aerden said, shaking his head. "Like a scary bedtime story or a way to keep the citizens in line. 'Don't go into the Black Hills alone. The stone guardians will come after you.' That kind of thing. They aren't real. Are they?"

"Stone guardians are very real," Andros said. "And incredibly dangerous. Our entire race was nearly wiped out by the war between the guardians five thousand years ago."

"I thought they were extinct," I said, barely finding my voice. "I thought they killed each other off in the war."

Andros shook his head. "Inside the libraries of the Underground, we have found many texts that reference the stone guardians as beings who come from another dimension. Just like the humans. There are many worlds besides these two, Lea. The stone guardians were not all killed. Those who survived were banished, the one remaining portal between their world and ours sealed and guarded for the last five thousand years."

"And you're telling me that somehow my father, the King of the North, has opened that portal? That's ridiculous. Why would he bring such a dangerous being back to our world? It doesn't make any sense."

My mind raced, searching my own memories for any reference my parents had ever made to stone guardians. The only thing I remembered was that the mines of magical gemstones scattered throughout the Shadow World were said to be the decayed bodies of these giant stone beings.

Diamonds were supposed to be the most powerful of all the gemstones. And the most rare. The symbol of the Order's High Priestess.

I touched a hand to the rope chain around my neck. The only true Shadow World diamond I had ever seen was embedded in a key Aerden had given me before he was kidnapped a hundred years ago. I had never been able to unlock its power, but I kept it with me at all times.

Could all these things be connected? Why would my father have brought a diamond stone guardian to his city? Were they even real?

Aerden was right. It sounded more like a myth than truth. There was nothing said about them that made me believe they were anything more than stories told in hushed whispers. Dark fairy tales meant to scare shadowlings into doing what they were told.

"Your father has been slipping into madness for years, Princess, and you know it," Andros said. "I have warned you many times that he was eventually going to do something that put us all in even more danger than we've already endured for so many years. Every chance he has had to fight back against the Order or to save his people, the king has turned his back on us. And it's only gotten worse over time. The King's Guard used to patrol the villages, keeping the Order's hunters away. He slowly reduced the patrols to one single unit of six soldiers for the entire Northern Kingdom. They were useless. They spent more of their time searching for the Resistance than for the actual hunters.

"When the King's Guard stopped their patrols, it seemed like a blessing. But then the doors to the gate around the King's City closed soon after, and we realized the king had given up on his subjects outside the city. He practically offered us to the Order on a silver platter. The fact that the doors closed right after the Order increased their recruiting can't be lost on you, can it?"

The anger in his tone grew as he spoke, and it kind of pissed me off. I knew what was coming next.

"So you come here to accuse me of turning my back on you as well, is that it? Is that what you're saying?" I stepped toward him. "You must know it is true if you're so quick to understand my meaning," he said, his eyes narrowing.

My jaw tensed. "No, I just know you that well," I said. "How do I know this story about the stone guardians isn't just your way of getting me to come home and fight for the Resistance?"

"Do you think I would lie about such things?"

"I think you would do whatever you thought necessary to achieve your goals."

"Is that not an honorable thing? Doing whatever it takes to save my people? Your people, Princess. Or have you forgotten where you come from? Who you are? Have you been living with these humans for so long you've forgotten where your duty truly lies?"

Anger boiled in my veins, its power so strong my body began shifting to the black smoke of my demon form. Tendrils of dark shadows swirled around my skin like snakes.

Aerden took a step toward me, but one glance warned him off. I regretted saying he could stay. If I had known what Andros was about to accuse my father of, I never would have let him say it in front of Aerden.

"I understand why you came here," Andros said, his voice softening. He raised his hands and stepped back, putting some distance between us. "I know you only did what you thought you had to do out of love. But what reason do you have to stay now? Jackson is engaged to another. Harper is the heir to her father's kingdom in the south and will soon take her place on his throne. Let them handle what is needed here in the human world and in the Southern Kingdom. Your people need you now more than ever. I'm begging you. If your father has brought a stone guardian into the King's City, then he has truly gone mad. He must believe the giant will protect him from the Order. It's the only explanation. The time has come, Princess. You cannot deny your place as queen any longer. Please, for the sake of your people, come home to claim your throne."

With this, he got down on one knee before me and lowered his head.

My anger dissipated, leaving behind fear and confusion.

Andros was right. I had only come to the human world because of Jackson. I followed him here because I loved him, and I foolishly believed that if I joined him in his quest to save his brother, he would someday return to me. That we would be married and have a life together.

There was a part of me that held onto that hope even after he fell in love with Harper. But now? When he asked me to release him from our engagement—to give back the heart stone he had given me one hundred years ago during our engagement ceremony—he broke my heart all over again.

Why would I choose to stay here with them, instead of returning to my homeland?

Tears stung the corners of my eyes, but I forced them back. I would not cry. I was stronger than that.

I lifted my head and motioned for Andros to stand.

"Tell me everything you know about stone guardians."

Sarra Cannon

I Didn't Know

Jackson

My visions were becoming more violent.

Sometimes I saw them clearly in my mind like flashes of memory, but other times I had to put pencil to paper to extract them from my brain. When a vision was struggling to be released, I often felt it like a fever. It was almost like a sickness that needed to be drawn out from me, the way surgeons used to use leeches to draw blood from patients.

Until it had shape and form, I had no hope of relief. And tonight, I had the fever.

I drew with my eyes closed, almost as if in a trance. My hands worked on their own, as if the visions were speaking directly to them, bypassing the rest of me in an effort to work more efficiently. I worked fast and hard, stopping only to tear my shirt from my body, sweat pouring from me.

Sometimes the visions held onto me for hours, my hands working through image after image, page after page, without pause. Tonight, there was a stack of nearly twenty pages already filled to the very edge with scenes of battle. Blood running through the streets of a small town. Swords raised against each other. Magic clashing in the air in a burst of light.

And a woman in a black hood. She was always there, but her face was never visible.

Some of tonight's drawings were a small piece of the scene shown in detail, like the side of someone's face with a streak of blood along their cheek. Others were more like silhouettes, drawn in sweeping strokes and dark shadows, but with no real detail.

The hooded woman was in every single drawing, but she always appeared like a ghost or a memory, see-through and shaded. A piece of her cloak, the profile of her hood, I drew them all, begging for my vision to show me her face or give some other clue. But none came.

Who was she?

It wasn't until I finally drew a panorama of the entire scene that my pencil fell to the desktop, my fingers cramped and twisted. I pushed away from the desk and stood for the first time in hours.

I walked to the window and looked back toward the bed where Harper slept. We had switched places at some point in the early morning hours. I couldn't sleep, but she was finally peaceful and quiet.

Lately, we both seemed to spend a lot of time staring out of this window. It was the place where our eyes had first locked onto each other, our souls connected in ways we couldn't have realized at the time.

Whenever I started to feel hopeless or afraid that the coming war would be too much for us, I thought of that first moment when I saw her, standing right here looking down at me. She had no idea just how important she was or how much we all needed her. And yet, when the time came, she was the only one strong enough to fight back.

The memory served as a reminder that there were still witches inside the Order who were pure of heart. Victims trapped under the tyranny of the four remaining sister priestesses.

It reminded me that even though my brother was free, there were still others who needed and deserved our help.

Despite the price yet to be paid.

I studied my final drawing, the pencil marks smudging at the edge of the paper under my thumb. I had drawn it with heartbreaking accuracy.

The Southern Kingdom. The domed city built by Harper's father, the King of the South, to protect his people from the Order. He had built it decades ago, inviting all who lived in his kingdom to join him inside the safety of the dome. Now, thousands lived there, all protected by the king's loyal soldiers and the magic of the dome that kept the Order's hunters out.

It was Harper's kingdom now. Harper's city.

And someday soon, the war would bring it down.

I crumpled the drawing in my fist and walked over to the desk with its stack of papers. I tossed them all in the trash can. I didn't want Harper to see this. She had enough to worry about without having to see it with her own eyes.

She whimpered, and I turned, crossing to her in seconds. At first, I thought my moving around had woken her up, but when I sat beside her on the bed, I saw that she was still sleeping.

Her face twisted into a frown and she whimpered again. Her chin jerked to the side, her hands curled into fists.

I touched her forehead. She was hot, her hair drenched in sweat.

"Harper," I said softly, gripping her fist with my own. I ran my hand across her cheek, trying not to startle her, but wanting to pull her from the nightmare.

Like my visions, she'd been feverish with dreams. She didn't like to talk about it, and I understood. I hadn't told her the truth about my drawings, either. If we didn't talk about our fears out loud, they weren't real yet.

And I had desperately wanted to enjoy the happiness of our engagement for just a few more days.

But I knew our time for pretending was up. Our months of peace were over, and something was coming for us.

I could feel the heat of the next vision already warming the blood in my veins. They were relentless, consuming my nights the way these nightmares often consumed her.

I'd hidden it from her longer than I ever should have, and man, was she going to be pissed.

Harper thrashed to the side, another cry escaping from her throat as she reached her hands out, holding onto my forearms.

"Harper," I said, louder this time. I wrapped my hands around her wrists and shook her slightly. "Wake up."

Her eyes opened and she drew in a strangled breath.

I pulled her into my arms and held her close to me.

"You're okay," I said softly. "I'm here. It was just a dream."

Hot tears fell onto my shoulder. Harper clung to me, crying as she struggled to catch her breath.

When she finally pulled away, her dark brown eyes were wide and her cheeks were flushed.

"What is it?" I asked in a whisper. "What happened?"

She took a breath and shook her head.

"Emeralds," she said. "I think someone's been trying to warn me."

My body tensed and grew suddenly ice-cold, as if a ghost were breathing down my neck. "Who?"

"I don't know," she said. She closed her eyes. "I've never seen her face, but she's there in every dream, Jackson. All this time, I thought she wanted to hurt me, but tonight, I got farther than I ever have before. I forced myself to keep going. She's tall and when she moves, it's like she's floating on air, just gliding over the surface instead of actually walking. I keep trying to see her face, but—"

"She's wearing a black cloak?"

Harper paused, lips slightly open. Her eyes widened and she stared at me for a long moment before the realization finally came to her. She released my arms and scooted back against her pillows, drawing her legs up to her chest.

"You've seen her, too," she said. It wasn't a question. Her gaze flicked to the desk.

"Yes." I waited for the anger. I knew better than to keep secrets from her, but all I wanted to do was protect her. Whenever I shared my visions with her in the past, we usually misinterpreted them, leading to unnecessary fear and worry. I didn't want to do that to her again. Not until I was sure what I was seeing.

"Do you know who she is?" she asked. There was sadness in her voice, but not anger.

Somehow, that was worse.

"I haven't been able to see her face, either," I said. "But she's in every single drawing."

"I want to see them." Harper stood and crossed to the desk.

I moved faster, quickly nudging between her and the notebook. I'd thrown tonight's drawings in the trash, but there were many more still inside my book. None as gruesome as tonight's, but I still didn't want her to see them.

"We don't know what they mean, anyway," I said. I placed a hand on her shoulder, but she twisted away. My heart tightened.

"After all this time, you still want to hide from me," she said. "I thought the memories you showed me last night before you proposed were supposed to change things between us. You said you wanted me to see you at your worst before I agreed to a lifetime together. And yet, here you are, still hiding the truth from me, because you think I can't handle it."

"That's not it at all," I said. "I only want to protect you. Seeing pieces of the future is my burden, Harper. Not yours."

Her eyes snapped to mine, the anger I'd been dreading blazing in her expression.

She stepped toward me and put one hand on the gold locket I'd given her. The other rose to my chest, covering my heart.

"We are one now, you and me," she said. "Our burden is the same. If we keep things from each other, how will we ever get through this? I don't want to be alone in this, Jackson. I want to know we're a team. You're always thinking about my heart, my fears. Always trying to protect me. But I want to protect you, too. You shouldn't bear this alone."

I put my hand on hers and closed the small gap of space that remained between us.

"I don't deserve you," I whispered, placing my lips against her forehead. She was still warm from the dream.

"Love isn't about deserving," she said. "It's about being completely open to each other. It's about needing and being needed. And I need you now more than ever. I think whoever this cloaked woman is, she's been trying to warn us that the emerald priestess is going to attack. I think it's going to happen soon. We need to be ready."

She pulled back slightly and searched my eyes.

"I need to see those drawings, Jackson."

I squeezed her hand and nodded.

I turned back toward my desk and leaned against the worn wood. I did not want to show her what I'd seen. The destruction would tear her apart, and no matter what we did, there was nothing that would change it. Her father's domed city was going to be destroyed and people were going to die.

It was only a matter of when.

Reluctantly, I opened the notebook and slid several drawings across the desk, spreading them out from bad to worst. Harper came around beside me, the soft fabric of her nightgown brushing against my side as she studied them.

Her eyes dipped to the trash can and before I could stop her, she took the crumpled paper from the bin and smoothed it out. Her knees buckled.

I caught her just before she hit the floor and cradled her in my arms. She rested her head against my chest, still clutching the drawing in her hand.

"I didn't know," she whispered through her tears. "I didn't know."

I held her close to me and rocked her back and forth.

My eyes drifted down to the page, seeing again the unavoidable destruction that was coming our way, focusing on the hooded figure in the corner, her face just out of sight.

More Than Ever

Harper

"Ten minutes," I shouted from the bottom of the stairs.

"I'm up," Mary Anne called back.

"Be there in a minute," Zara sang, her white-blonde hair hanging down as she leaned over the balcony.

Someone yelled a curse word and seemed to stumble and crash into something. I laughed. Probably Mary Anne. She hated mornings.

Jackson ran down the stairs. "Good morning, gorgeous," he said. He pulled a fresh black t-shirt over his head and then kissed me on the cheek.

We walked back toward the kitchen together. Mordecai, Joost, Erick, and Cristo—demons demons who had originally come through to the human world with Lea about thirty years ago—were already sitting at the large farm table by the back door. The plates of bacon, eggs, and pancakes I'd set in front of them a few minutes ago had already been devoured.

"Hungry much?" I asked with a laugh.

"Perfect hangover cure," Joost said, raising a glass of orange juice. "Thanks."

"Did you guys leave anything for the rest of us?" Jackson teased. He stole the only remaining piece of bacon off Cristo's plate.

"Hey," Cristo yelled, standing and swiping at Jackson's hand. He missed and the bacon disappeared into Jackson's mouth.

"Mmm," he said with his mouth full. "Delicious."

I rolled my eyes and turned back to the stove. With a wave of my hand, the spatula rose off the counter and flipped the pancakes. A fork moved through the air to pull the bacon off the pan. With my other hand, I directed the large pitcher of orange juice to fill six more glasses waiting on the counter.

"You're getting so good at that," Jackson said. He downed a glass of OJ and started filling his plate with food.

"With this many people living here, I had no choice," I said. "It was either that or let you guys starve."

"Who's starving?" Mary Anne asked from the hallway. "Please tell me the demons didn't eat all the food again."

She peeked her head around the corner and her shoulders relaxed.

"Thank God." She grabbed two plates and tossed a couple of pancakes on each of them.

Essex, her demon boyfriend, followed behind her, grabbing the extra plate from her and heading over to the table. "Thank you for this meal, Harper," he said, taking a second to bow toward me before he sat down. "I am most grateful."

"You're welcome," I said. I shot a glance at the four demons closest to the door and raised an eyebrow. "See how easy it is to say thank-you?"

Erick stood and smacked the back of Cristo's head. "Yeah, man, where are your manners?"

"Mine?" Cristo said. He stood and chased Erick around to the other side of the table.

A blue butterfly fluttered into the room. Zara shifted back to her human form and giggled. "Good morning, everyone."

She took a few steps and then seemed to stumble over her own feet. She caught the edge of the counter and paused.

"Are you okay?" I asked.

She shook her head, worry flashing in her pale blue eyes for a moment. It wasn't a look I was used to seeing from her.

"I'm fine," she said, clearing her throat.

But when she pushed her white-blonde hair back from her face, a dark streak of black underneath caught my eye.

"What's this?" I asked, moving to touch it.

She pulled away and readjusted her hair to cover it. "Nothing," she said, her smile forced and flustered.

"I knew you always wanted to be more like me, but I don't think you can pull off the goth look, so don't even think about it," Mary Anne teased as she walked toward the table.

Zara laughed, but it wasn't her normal, carefree giggle. It sounded scared. I was going to ask her more about it, but Courtney and Aerden came through the door at that moment and grabbed some empty seats up at the counter. I floated three plates over and spooned eggs onto them.

"We've got less than five minutes before we need to leave for school," I said. "Where's Lea?"

Aerden shrugged, but a weird expression crossed his face before he could hide it. Guilt slipped through my stomach like a venomous snake.

I had heard them outside, training late into the night. I knew she was upset, and I completely understood it, but that didn't mean I had to like it.

I reached a hand up and slid Jackson's engagement locket under the neck of my shirt. I hated the thought of what Lea must be going through. And I hated the fact that I was going to have to tone down my own happiness when it was the one thing that got me out of bed this morning.

But this is what it was to have twelve people living in the same house. Well, technically eight demons, three witches, and one half-breed. Every once in a while, you had to make sacrifices for the good of the group.

I needed to do whatever it took to make Lea feel comfortable. If she needed her space, I'd give it to her. I wouldn't even say a word about her training in the woods, even though she knew I hated it.

29

Right now, more than ever, we needed each other.

I took a deep breath and tried to ignore the fear that knotted inside me when I thought of the war waiting for us on the horizon. I piled the remaining food on a plate and turned back to the group, planting a smile on my face.

"Who wants more pancakes?" I asked.

"Me," Erick, Joost, and Mordecai all said at the same time.

Everyone piled into the white van. It used to say Shadowford Home for Girls on the side of it, but after I'd taken the house back for myself and invited my friends to live here with me, we'd decided to paint it fresh. Now, it had an ice-covered lightning bolt down the side, a joke from the demon guys one crazy night this past summer. It was kind of growing on me.

Before Erick and the others climbed in, I held them back and slid the door closed.

"Would you guys mind missing school today?" I asked.

"What? Miss a riveting day of human high school? I can't bear the thought," Cristo said.

I smacked him on the arm. "I'm being serious. I need you to do something for me."

"Anything," Mordecai said, his black dreads sweeping his shoulders.

"Go through to the domed city and just keep an eye out," I said. "Make sure the guards are all on alert and patrolling the area throughout the day."

Mordecai's eyes grew dark. "What's happened?"

"Nothing, yet," I said. "Can you do it?"

"Of course," he said.

The four of them shifted and headed toward our secret portal near the lake.

It wasn't unusual for them to be missing a few days of school. We had gotten good enough at altering records and memories here in town that it didn't matter anyway.

Sometimes, they went out of town, splitting up to go help demons who had been freed from the sapphire gates acclimate to the human world. When we killed Priestess Winter, we performed a ritual that broke the Peachville demon gate and freed all the demons and witches attached to it.

Afterward, when things settled down, we started the large task of going around to all of the remaining sapphire gates throughout the world, performing the same ritual. It had taken two full months of nonstop work over the summer, and after school started, the four demon guys had helped pick up the pieces.

Most of the demons who went free chose to return home to their families in the Shadow World, but some wanted to stay here in the human world, feeling that they had nothing left to go home to. Either their families had all been abducted by another color gate or they simply felt too broken to face their past. They all had their reasons, and we respected their wishes, helping them find jobs and homes when we could.

A lot of the witches from the sapphire gates had been angry, which made the transition even more difficult. The Order of Shadows had a lot of flaws—to say the least—but many witches loved the unstoppable power their demon slaves gave them.

Witches were recruited young and trained in basic magic. In demon gate towns, cheerleading teams served as the front for the Order's recruiting program. After school, instead of practicing cheers, though, they retreated to a secret room inside the gym to practice basic spells and learn the history of the Order. Most of them came from long lines of witches and simply followed in their mothers' footsteps. When they turned eighteen, though, they were officially inducted into the Order.

For most, this was a terrifying and eye-opening experience. They were dragged down into a ritual room below ground, naked, and placed above the portal stone, the binding ritual pulling a kidnapped Shadow Demon through the portal and forcing them inside the body of the young witch.

The demons became slaves to the witches from that moment forward, bound together, the demon's essence acting as a type of battery for the witch's power, making them many times more powerful than they otherwise would have been.

At first, a lot of witches rebelled against the idea of having a demon locked inside of them. Over time, though, most became addicted to it. Greed was a powerful sin, and when you could use unlimited glamours to make yourself beautiful, and had practically unlimited power to get anything you wanted, most initiates accepted the Order's ways.

Our ritual to free those demons meant stealing power from the witches, and the majority of them didn't like it much. Some fought back, but with the demons on our side and the witches' strength weakened, we had been able to kill most rebellions before they truly started.

It had been a chaotic and exhausting summer, but when the last of the sapphire gates had been closed, we had all returned here to Peachville, turning what once was Shadowford Home for Girls back into Brighton Manor, the home of my family for generations.

Courtney had been an orphan like me, brought here by the Order when they were searching for their lost Prima, the head witch of the coven. Which turned out to be me. Mary Anne, a member of an ancient race of crow witches, had been sent here disguised as an orphan for the same reason, the Mother Crow hoping to find and kill me so that she could transfer the power of my bloodline to her own.

Zara, the youngest daughter of Priestess Winter, had left her home in Washington, DC to join us here after her mother died. The four of us were the only humans living here, although I was also half-demon on my father's side.

Mordecai, Joost, Erick, and Cristo were some of Lea's best friends. They lived at Brighton Manor off and on, depending on whether they were needed by other demons.

Essex and Mary Anne had fallen in love back in the Shadow World when we had been hiding out there last year. Jackson, Lea, and Aerden completed our group of twelve.

Most weekdays, we piled into the van and went to school, but we had three full training days a week when we descended into the secret training room below the gym and practiced our magic.

Today was a training day.

I looked up at the house. Lea had never shown for breakfast, and I asked Jackson if we should wait for her.

"I don't want to be late for school today," I said.

Jackson looked back at Aerden, but he shrugged. "Just go," Jackson said. "If she wants to come, she'll meet us there. She has her bike."

I bit my lower lip and nodded, climbing into the driver's seat and closing the door. All of the demons had motorcycles, which continued to surprise me. I guess it was just the cool thing to do when you were a demon. Maybe someday I would get one for myself. Lord knows, Jackson looked sexy on his.

I put the van into drive and pulled away from the house.

With the warning of a possible attack from the emerald priestess, the last place in the world I wanted to be was Peachville High School, but it was the best way for us to keep up our skills.

Since the demons in our group needed some kind of life force to pull from in order to cast here in the human world, Zara had taken clippings from the gardens and grown vines and flowers all along the walls in our training room. They were mostly destroyed by the end of a session, but she was able to grow them back in less than a day, meaning they were ready to go as a source of fuel the next time we met.

Also, with hundreds of students practically above our heads, the demons in our group could pull from them without making a noticeable difference.

No one had any idea about this room besides us. My half-sister, Angela King, had been the Order's training coach, in charge of the cheerleading squad for years. Other than the higher-ups in the coven, she was the only one who knew about this room. And those higher-ups had either been killed by the Order or had died in the battle.

Angela still taught English classes here at the school and when she could, she joined us down in the training room.

Today was a Monday, which meant we only had to show up for homeroom and then we could retreat to the gym. When we parked and walked into the school, I headed straight for Angela's classroom.

She was standing in front of her desk, talking to a student, and when she saw me, her face broke out into a huge smile. She excused herself and came over to meet me in the doorway. She wrapped her arms around me.

"I'm so excited for you," she said. "Congratulations again on your engagement."

"Shhh," I said, pretending to be worried someone would hear her. "A senior in high school engaged? What will everyone think?"

She laughed. "As if you care," she said. "Are you training this morning?"

"Yes," I said. "Can you get away?"

She looked toward the ceiling, as if her schedule were written there. "Not today," she said. "My schedule is packed." Her features darkened. "Is everything okay?"

"No," I said, wishing I had a different answer to that question. "I mean, I'm fine, but I have reason to believe the castle and the domed city might be attacked soon."

She looked behind her and closed her door, shutting us out in the hallway where there were less ears to hear.

"Harper, what's going on? Why would you think that?"

"I've been having these dreams," I said. "And Jackson's visions line up with it, everything pointing to the emerald priestess attacking the dome."

"When?"

"I don't know. Soon, I think," I said. "What should we do?"

Technically our father had left the kingdom to me, but Angela was older than I was, and we had basically shared the responsibility.

"I'll talk to someone and see if I can get a substitute for the rest of the week," she said. "I'll pack my things and head to the dome in the morning."

"Thank you," I said. "I'm going to visit Eloise in Cypress. I would think she'd have contacted me if she'd heard anything, but I want to warn her to be on alert, just in case."

The bell rang and several students pushed past us, saying good morning to my sister. No one here knew she was my half-sister. We shared the same demon father, but had different mothers, a secret that had been well kept for a very long time until I'd discovered the truth earlier this year.

She was all the family I had left. By blood, anyway. And she meant the world to me. What I had seen in Jackson's drawings affected her as much as it did me, and she needed to know what was coming.

"I've got to run, but keep me updated, okay?"

She nodded, her dark layers spilling over her cheeks. She pushed them back behind her ears and gave me a quick hug before returning to her classroom full of students.

I adjusted my backpack and made a run for my homeroom.

Sarra Cannon

Point Made

Aerden

I sat on a stool in the corner, watching as the others threw everything they had at Zara.

She looked like some kind of little fairy, hovering a few feet above the air, her legs folded beneath her. She wore a blindfold, and her hands rested against her knees, palms up.

Zara's focus was amazing. She had Harper, Jackson, Courtney, and Essex all throwing various types of magical attacks her way, but she never once showed any sign of fear or hesitation. Her face was entirely at peace, her shoulders relaxed.

She sat in the middle of her four assailants, blocking each of their attacks with such precision, she didn't waste an ounce of her own energy. It was effortless and beautiful to watch. Fire, ice, lightning. None of it could touch her. Instead of one large shield around her entire body, she sensed the attacks just before they landed, creating a tiny pinpoint light that absorbed the magic.

Lately, she had even learned to not only absorb the magic, but to deflect it, sending it back toward her attacker.

I had never seen someone so young have such control and focus.

But there was a flaw in her defense that no one else seemed to see. It was obvious to me every time I watched them do this particular exercise, but in most of our training sessions, I opted to sit back and watch.

Casting magic wasn't something I was ready for yet, and I didn't want to have to explain myself to anyone else.

I could feel some of the others becoming impatient with me. My brother in particular. When we were shadowlings, we'd sparred together often, both with physical weapons and with magic. Back then, we were evenly matched, or so it seemed.

As we grew older, he was being groomed to take over the Northern Kingdom someday at Lea's side. He'd spent most of his days in a classroom, learning politics and history.

I was being trained to take over command of the royal guard. Unlike Jackson, my classroom was constant battle and training in all forms of combat. I had a natural talent with the element of fire, but for some reason, I'd always been drawn to physical weaponry. Staffs, swords, and most of all, my axe.

God, I missed my axe.

It was this enormous silver battle-axe that took two hands to wield. Well, until I'd grown strong enough to lift it with just one arm. As my strength grew, so did my skill. Hell, I'd been graceful with that thing, when most demons who tried to so much as lift it got thrown off balance.

There was just something about wrapping my fist around a great weapon and swinging it with all my might. Anyone could stand fifty feet away and throw a magical fireball at a target, but to swing a heavy axe like that took strength and agility and incredible skill. I'd spent more hours than I could count working with that axe until I'd mastered it.

When I got kidnapped and brought to the human world, I had no control over my own form. I was trapped in shadow, but not even that. I was less than a shadow. I was a pool of energy and thought. A slave.

For a hundred years, I had lived like that, with no ability to hold a weapon in my hand. Magic was all I had, and it was never my own to cast.

Since I'd been freed, I just didn't feel like it anymore. I longed for the feel of a solid weapon in my hand. I loved the way my muscles felt as they stretched and flexed.

It was something everyone else in this room took for granted. They saw physical weapons as archaic. But watching them today, throwing every type of magic they could think of toward Zara without being able to so much as alter a hair on her head, I suddenly felt like it was time for me to show them the power of a physical weapon when you were battling against magical beings.

No one noticed as I slid off the stool and reached for a small pebble that had chipped off a nearby brick. It was a tiny thing, barely two ounces in my palm.

I gripped it between my thumb and forefinger, aimed, and sent it flying through the air toward Zara.

The pebble hit her square on the nose. I suppressed a smile as her eyelids snapped open and her hand rose to rub the stinging part. She lost concentration and fell to the cement floor, one of Jackson's icy spears barely missing her shoulder.

Everyone stopped and turned toward me, their mouths open like they'd never seen someone throw a pebble before.

I raised an eyebrow, shrugged, and turned back to my stool in the corner.

Point made.

Keep Your Eyes Open

Harper

I left for Cypress right after school.

It was a four-hour drive, so I called Eloise before I left to let her know to expect me late. She promised to have dinner waiting and told me to be careful.

Sometimes the inability to use the doors inside the attic at Brighton Manor was frustrating, but we had no idea if the Order was still monitoring the Hall of Doorways. As far as I knew, the home of every Prima had a hallway like ours—a long corridor with doors lining both sides as far as the eye could see. The doors allowed members of the Order to travel across the world in just a few steps, going from a Prima's house in Georgia all the way to one in Paris. All you had to do was know which door you were looking for.

If I'd wanted to, I could have simply gone into the attic of my own house, found Eloise's door in Cypress, and walked straight through. It would have taken less than five minutes.

But if the Order was somehow watching our door and keeping track of who went where, my actions could put Eloise in danger. I couldn't risk it.

Of course, I wondered if our alliance with Cypress was even a secret at this point. Eloise and her two daughters, Meredith and Caroline, were dear friends of mine. During a visit to Peachville when I was still a cheerleader in training for the Order, Caroline was abducted by a group of crow-shifting witches. She was almost killed, and when I saved her, a piece of Cypress's demon was transferred into me, giving me some of his abilities and powers.

The connection I shared with them was deeper than could be explained.

Eloise and her daughters had fought with us in the battle against Priestess Winter, and we had no way of knowing whether anyone involved in that fight had survived and told the Order about their betrayal. So far, no one had come to Eloise to ask her about the fight, and we were hoping our alliance was still unknown to the other priestesses.

If an attack was coming, though, she needed to know about it.

"Harper, I'm so happy you're here," Eloise said as she ushered me into her home a few hours later. She glanced around the quiet neighborhood. "Where's your car?"

"I parked a couple blocks over, just in case." I shrugged out of my backpack and hoodie and slung them over my arm. I'd worn all black, covered my hair in a hoodie, and stuck to the shadows.

Eloise stared at my clothes, a worried expression flashing in her eyes.

"This isn't just a friendly visit, is it?" she asked. "What's happened?"

"Nothing. Yet." I tried to keep the fear out of my voice, but I couldn't hide anything from her. Eloise had become like a mother to me, which was something I wasn't used to since I never met my real mother. It was strange to feel so open with a woman her age. Life in the foster care system had caused me to distrust every adult who said they cared about me. Inevitably, they'd always abandoned me or abused me.

But Eloise was one of the most giving, caring women I'd ever known.

I needed her advice right now, but I was so scared that I was putting her in danger just by being here. If the emerald priestess was really the next sister to come after us, though, Eloise might already be in more trouble than any of us realized.

"Come into the kitchen," she said. "I've got dinner waiting."

"Are the girls here?" I asked, glancing up the stairs as we walked back toward the kitchen.

"Meredith is at school until Thanksgiving break, but Caroline and Sophie are upstairs doing homework," she said. "I know Caroline is dying to see you, but I told her to give us some time to talk first."

"Good," I said. I sat down at the elegant table, and Eloise placed a plate of spaghetti in front of me. "Thank you. This looks delicious."

I twisted a few noodles on my fork and took a bite. I loved Eloise's cooking. It was really nice to be having a quiet meal that I didn't have to help cook for once. I loved my life at Brighton Manor, but sometimes it got a little loud and chaotic.

"Why are you really here, Harper?" she asked, sitting down across from me with her own plate and a glass of wine. "I thought maybe you were here to share some good news of a more personal nature."

I looked up at her and she smiled, one eyebrow raised.

I couldn't help but touch the golden locket I wore around my neck. "How did you know?" I asked, unable to suppress a smile of my own.

"Jackson told me a few weeks ago what he was planning," she said. "The girls and I really wanted to be there at your Halloween party, but I thought maybe it was best we stay away from Peachville for a while."

I bit my lower lip and set my fork back onto my plate. "Has something happened here?" I asked. "Something that would make you think it was bad to come to us?"

She drew a long breath in and straightened her shoulders. "I didn't want to worry you," she said. "But yes, a few things have happened in the past week."

My stomach twisted. "Tell me."

"Someone came to the house," she said. "It was a woman I'd never seen before, but she wore a necklace with a very large square emerald pendant. She introduced herself as Lauralei Welton, and said she had come on behalf of the priestess who had once controlled all the emerald demon gates. Power has shifted again, Harper, and the emerald priestess—Priestess Evers—is going to take back control of the emerald gates now that her sister is dead."

I closed my eyes and pressed my palms against the table to steady myself.

"So now you're directly under the rule of the emerald priestess?" I asked. It definitely didn't seem like a coincidence.

"Yes," she said. "I've never officially seen or met her, but she was the priestess in charge when my mother and grandmother were Prima here in Cypress. From what I've heard about her, she was not a very nice woman."

"None of them are," I said. "How can they be when they do such horrible things?"

"She's also quite a bit more secretive," Eloise said. "In my grandmother's journals, she only mentions the emerald priestess visiting Cypress three times. Priestess Winter used to come here nearly once a month. Apparently, the emerald priestess has a daughter she's incredibly fond of who usually comes in her place."

"What did she come for back then? Did your grandmother say?"

Eloise swallowed and dabbed a napkin at her mouth. She avoided my eyes for a moment, and I got this terrible sick feeling inside.

"She only came to visit when she wanted to punish someone," she said. She stood and walked over to a desk built into the counter on the other side of the room. She opened the top drawer and took out a book with a green leather cover.

"My grandmother Iris's journal," she said, sliding it across the table toward me. "You can take it with you. It might give you some insight into the emerald priestess. Back then, she was called Ashlynn Evers. I'm not sure what she goes by now."

"Her real name is Hazel," I said, running a hand along the smooth leather surface of the journal. We learned the hard way that the five priestess sisters had figured out a way to cheat death, eating the souls of their oldest daughters to stay alive. "Thank you for this. Anything we can learn about her is incredibly important right now."

"I'll help however I can. There's still so much to learn about the Order," she said. "Until you discovered the truth about Priestess Winter being one of the actual original founding members of the Order, none of us had any idea she was two hundred years old. She looked so young, and her appearance and name changed each time she pretended to switch from one life to the next. I still get chills every time I think about what that woman did to her own daughters."

I did, too.

And I was pretty sure the other priestesses used the same practice.

"Did any of the other Primas in your family keep a journal?" I asked. "Anyone from when the emerald priestess was in control of this gate?"

"Not that I know of," she said. "My mother gave me this one just before she died. I've never found any other journals in the house. So as far as I know, my grandmother was the only one."

I nodded and slipped the green journal into my backpack.

"What else did the woman who came here have to say?" I asked. "You said her name was Lauralei?"

"Yes. She didn't say much else. Only that we were now expected to answer to Priestess Evers, and she would soon be coming to visit us."

I raised my head, my heart skipping a beat. "Did she say when?"

Eloise shook her head.

"If you find out when to expect her, and you can get a message to me, please let me know," I said. "I have a terrible feeling something bad is about to happen. I've been having these dreams. A woman in a dark cloak keeps coming to me, trying to tell me something about the emerald priestess."

Eloise put her hand on mine. "Harper, maybe your fears are getting the best of you."

I shook my head. "It's more than that, Eloise," I said. "I think she's been planning something for months. I know it's just a dream, but it feels like so much more. I think it's a warning. That's why this visit from one of her witches scares me," I said. "She's taking back control over what she feels is rightfully hers—the emerald gates. Somehow, she's planning to use that against us."

Eloise's face grew pale. "Do you think she's somehow found out about the alliance?"

"I don't know," I said. "But we need to warn everyone who has joined our alliance to be careful. Can you find out if they've all received a similar visit from this Lauralei person?"

She nodded.

When we first defeated Priestess Winter, we decided to call ourselves the Demon Liberation Movement. We committed ourselves to defeating the Order and had all decided we would target the emerald priestess next. In order to defeat her, we knew it was in our best interest to convince as many emerald gates as possible to secretly join our cause.

This had been a tough assignment. Many of the witches in the Order liked the power their demon slaves gave them, and they would do anything to protect their gates because of it. But there were others, like Eloise, who hated what the Order did to both demons and to young witches who were forced to join the Order without really knowing what that meant until it was too late.

When a witch was initiated, she not only had to adjust to a demon living inside her body, but she was also given a specific mission for her life. Girls who had dreamed of going to college and becoming doctors were told they needed to be teachers instead. Girls who had boyfriends they loved were told to break off those relationships and convince another, more powerful man to fall in love with them.

This was how the Order worked. In exchange for the power, beauty, and riches they offered, they also demanded your complete loyalty and lifelong service to their cause.

If you disobeyed them, the consequences were often deadly.

One of our missions over the past few months had been to seek out witches who were bound to the emerald gates who wanted out of the Order. This had meant sending some of our own into these communities to make friends and ask dangerous questions.

So far, we had managed to bring a total of six emerald demon gates into our alliance, including Cypress. Not every witch in these demon gate towns knew about the alliance, but anyone the Prima felt could be trusted was in on it.

It was a risky plan, but if it came to a war between us and the emerald priestess, we knew that having these gates on our side would be extremely valuable.

"It's possible someone in our alliance told the emerald priestess about us," I said. "That could be why she's planning some kind of attack. Until we know for sure, though, we need to make sure everyone knows to be on the lookout for anything strange. If they feel they're in danger, they know what to do."

Eloise pulled a ruby stone from her pocket and set it on the table. It was small stone, the size of a pea. I had given one to her and to each of the Primas in our new alliance.

"If something happens and you're attacked, or you feel like the emerald priestess knows about the alliance, rub your thumb across the top of the stone three times and hold it in your palm," I reminded her. "When it begins to glow, that means I am holding my stone as well, and we can speak through it."

She gave me a small smile. "I still don't understand exactly why the magic works, but it's brilliant," she said.

"I just hope we never have to use it."

The ruby communication stones were something we had learned about during our stay in the Underground. The stones allowed us to speak with each other across long distances without being detected, but they could only be used once.

I had given them to the six Primas in our alliance in case they needed our help. I had six matching stones that I carried with me at all times.

"What else can I do to help?" she asked.

"Just keep your eyes open," I said. "And be careful. It might be awhile before I come back to see you. I don't want to risk revealing our alliance if they don't already know about it."

She nodded, brushing a tear away from her eye.

"You said there were a couple of strange things going on?"

"Oh, Harper. There's been troubling news from one of my friends who went into hiding after the sapphire gates fell," she said. "Her daughter was kidnapped. She said a lot of the sapphire gates' trainees had been taken on Halloween night."

"Oh my God," I said. I closed my eyes and let my head fall into my hands. "They have no idea who took them or why?"

"No. They just disappeared without a trace," she said. "Everyone's terrified. Do you think there's anything you can do?"

"We'll start looking into it, I promise."

Something deep in my stomach knotted up. The dreams. The visions. Now this. It was all adding up to something terrible.

"I really should get going," I said. "It's late and it's a long drive home."

"I wish you could stay longer, but I understand," she said.

She reached for my hand across the table and squeezed.

"Oh," she said, jumping up. "I almost forgot."

She disappeared into the hallway and came back a few seconds later with a small box wrapped in gold paper.

"Happy birthday," she said with a smile. She sat down in the chair next to me and put the box on the table in front of me.

I bit my lower lip to hide a smile. "You didn't have to get me anything."

"Open it," she said. She placed a hand over her heart, a sweet expression in her eyes.

I tore the side of the pretty gold wrapping paper and lifted the top off a beautiful white satin box.

Inside, nestled in tissue paper, was a wedding veil attached to a diamond tiara.

Tears welled in my eyes, and I brought a hand to my mouth. "Was this yours?"

"Yes." She fingered the delicate lace, a dreamy look in her eyes. "Edward and I were married twenty years ago this December. It's hard to believe how fast the time flies."

She swiped a finger under her lashes.

"You've become like one of my own daughters, Harper," she said. "I know your mother never got to have a wedding of her own, but if she had, I'm sure she would have wanted you to have something to remember her by. It doesn't make up for what you've lost, but hopefully it will remind you that you are greatly loved."

Tears fell freely down my cheeks, and I stood to hug her with both arms.

"This means so much to me," I said. "Thank you."

"I wasn't sure if you'd be wearing a crown by then or if there were other demon traditions you'd want to honor, but—"

"It's perfect," I said. "We haven't even thought about preparations for the wedding, and if there really is an attack coming soon, I think it might be awhile before we can even think about it, but I'm sure that when the time comes, I'll want to honor both the human and demon sides of my heritage."

We held each other for a long time before we parted, both of us crying like babies.

"This means more to me than you can know," I said.

"I love you, Harper. You deserve so much happiness," she said.

"Someday, when all this is over and the Order is defeated, we will celebrate with a wedding," I said.

"Oh, my sweet girl, don't delay your own joy for them," she said. "No matter how hard you fight, there will always be suffering in this world. That's part of the balance of life. If you focus too much on the sorrow, what are you really fighting for, anyway?"

I smiled and ran my fingers across the lace of the veil.

"And you're sure Caroline and Meredith won't mind?" I asked. "I can give it back to them if they want to wear it at their own weddings, someday."

"Trust me, I don't plan on getting married anytime soon," Caroline said from the doorway of the kitchen.

I threw my arms open and she came running toward me, nearly knocking me over.

"I've been dying to see you," she said. "Did you really get engaged? Let me see the ring."

She pulled my hands toward her and then frowned, touching the only ring I'd ever worn, a sapphire I'd taken from the hunters in the Shadow World.

I laughed and showed her the locket, instead. "In Shadow Demon tradition, they don't exchange diamond rings like we do," I said. "They give something called a heart stone."

"Can I see it?" she asked, touching her fingers to the locket.

"It's locked inside and can only be seen by the person you're engaged to."

"How does it work?"

"Well, in their tradition, they take a clear stone similar to a diamond and place it near their heart. When they think of the person they're going to marry, their true feelings for them are transferred into the stone as pure light. The brighter the light, the more pure and true the love that shines from it."

Caroline sighed. "That's incredibly romantic," she said.

"Yeah, as long as you see a bright light." A young girl about Caroline's age came around from behind her and leaned against the doorframe. "Was yours bright?"

"Hi, Sophie," I said. "How are things going for you here in Cypress?"

She shrugged and rolled her eyes. "As good as can be expected," she said, a slight French accent coloring her words. "School is boring and all the boys are stupid, but other than that, I guess I can't complain."

I glanced at Eloise and she shook her head and turned away.

Sophie was sort of a refugee here in Cypress. She was the daughter of a Prima in a sapphire demon gate town in a small city in France. When we went over there to perform our ritual, a battle had broken out between some of the demons who had gone free and the witches who didn't want to let them go.

Nearly everyone in Sophie's coven had died, including her mother and two sisters.

We had found her alone in her mother's house, crying and covered in blood. It was horrifying. I had wanted to take her home to Brighton Manor with us, but Eloise offered to take her instead, promising me that Sophie would have a much more normal life here with her.

I had meant to come by and check on her more often, but life had been so busy. Between managing school, trying to help demons and witches from the freed sapphire gates find their place in the new world, and researching anything we could find on the remaining priestesses of the Order, I'd only been by twice since she moved in with Eloise.

"I'm sure the heart stone Jackson gave Harper was the brightest one ever," Caroline said. "I've never seen two people more in love."

I smiled and hugged Caroline again. "It was bright," I whispered.

"I knew it," she said. "But I still think he should have to get you a ring."

"We'll see." I grabbed my backpack off the floor and placed the box with the veil inside. "I'm sorry to have to leave already, but it's a long drive home, and I still have to be up for school in the morning."

"I'll see you out," Eloise said.

I hugged Caroline one last time and made her promise to text her older sister Meredith a hello from me. She and Sophie said goodnight and bounded back up the stairs to finish their homework.

At the door, Eloise paused. "One more thing," she said. "You never told me who you think the woman in the cloak is. The one from your dream."

I put my sweatshirt back on and pulled the hood over my head to hide my face.

"I have no idea," I said. I didn't tell her about Jackson's visions of the same woman. I didn't want to have to explain what else I'd seen in those drawings. "But whoever she is, I think she's trying to help."

"I hope you're right," she said. "Just be careful, Harper. Don't trust anyone completely."

"I know," I said. "That's a lesson I've had to learn the hard way."

"Once your eyes are opened to the true world around us, trust is the hardest thing to come by," she said.

"That's why I'm so glad I found you."

She smiled and hugged me close. "I love you," she said. "Don't stay away too long."

I nodded and slipped out into the cool evening air, hoping the next time I came to see her, we would be closer to finding a way to free her from the Order.

What We'd Been Afraid Of

Harper

I walked through the front door of Brighton Manor well after midnight. I thought of the delicate white box in my bag, and held back tears of gratitude. I may not have gotten a chance to know my real mother, but the relationship I had with Eloise was strong, and I was grateful every day for her presence in my life.

Jackson and I hadn't had a chance to talk about wedding plans, but holding the first piece of my wedding attire in my arms made me giddy.

I had never been the kind of girl who dreamed about her wedding, and I was never naive enough to believe I'd have a father who would walk me down the aisle or be able to look down from the steps of some chapel at my mother, dabbing a tissue at her eyes. That was the kind of fantasy reserved for romance novels and romantic movies. It was never going to my reality, and I had come to terms with that a long time ago.

But making this promise to the man I loved and building a family of our own together was the greatest dream of my life.

Maybe Eloise was right. Maybe we shouldn't wait for this war to be over to start thinking about the ceremony. Maybe it would be better to start planning something right away. It might be good to focus on something happy for a change.

Part of me wanted to go to the living room and get on one of the old laptops to start looking at wedding gowns, but there was still so much work to be done. I needed to read through Eloise's grandmother's journal for any clues about the real emerald priestess.

With Priestess Winter, we had at least known who she was and where she lived. Her other sisters had not been as easy to find.

Zara knew more information than anyone. As a third daughter, she'd been trained in magic and battle, groomed to take over as her mother's guardian when she got older. That's how I had first met her, actually. When my life as the future Prima of Peachville was threatened by an outside group, she had been sent here to protect me.

And when she'd learned the truth of her mother's nature, she had joined our side, fighting with us against her own family.

The information she'd learned as a child was extremely valuable to us now. She had been able to tell us that the citrine priestess in control of the European gates was Priestess Alexandra, the youngest of the five sisters. She lived in Italy and Zara had even visited her a couple of times, though they used the Hall of Doorways to get there, so she wasn't exactly sure how to get there without the doors. Still, the fact that she even knew which door to use was valuable to us since we still had a working hallway in our house.

But Zara's knowledge of the other three sisters was limited. She had met them a few times, but it was so easy for the priestesses to change their appearance that we couldn't rely on that to find them.

All we did know for certain was that four out of the five original sisters who created the Order two hundred years ago were still alive and ruling the Order today, and that a mysterious High Priestess seemed to rule over them all in some way.

Beyond a few details, though, we knew almost nothing.

I paused outside a room on the right. This used to be Mrs. Shadowford's living quarters. She used to run the girls' home here.

Now that Mrs. Shadowford was gone, we had turned these rooms into our battle headquarters. All the information we'd gathered about the various gates and priestesses was in these two rooms.

I stared at a large map of the world we'd put up on the wall. We'd used color-coded pushpins to mark demon gates in each of the five gemstone colors: sapphire, emerald, citrine, amethyst, and ruby. We had some knowledge that there might also be diamond gates somewhere, ruled by the High Priestess herself, but if they existed, we had yet to find them.

My eyes sought out the green pins, studying their locations and trying to find some type of pattern. There had to be a reason why one gate was chosen as an emerald gate and another was more suited to sapphire. But what? And did it really matter?

These were the types of questions that kept me up at night. Sometimes I thought that if I could unravel the secrets of the Order's creation and discover their methods for choosing one place over another or one stone over another, it might unlock all kinds of opportunities for us to understand and hunt them down.

Like sapphire, the majority of emerald gates were here in the United States. I felt certain the emerald priestess's home portal had to be somewhere nearby, as well. We just had to find it. Once we knew where to find her, we could finally begin piecing together a plan to kill her and free the emerald gates, just as we had done for the sapphire ones.

If we could just attack her before she had the chance—

"Harper?"

I jumped slightly at Mary Anne's voice. "You scared me," I said, laughing. "I thought everyone would be asleep by now."

"Essex and I were up playing video games," she said. "He just went up to bed, and I was about to grab a snack in the kitchen. Wanna join me?"

"Sure," I said. "I'm starving."

"I thought you were eating at Eloise's?"

We walked to the kitchen and Mary Anne grabbed a bowl of grapes from the fridge.

"She made spaghetti," I said. "But we got to talking and I just kind of lost my appetite."

"Ooh, you should have told her to wrap it up for you," she said. "I love her spaghetti."

"Me, too."

I made myself a peanut butter and jelly sandwich and joined Mary Anne at the table. I put my backpack on the chair next to me and smiled at the thought of the white box inside.

"What are you smiling about?" she asked. "You look like the cat who ate the canary."

I put my sandwich down and opened the backpack. I carefully removed the white box and slid it toward her.

"What's this?"

I smiled again, my cheeks warming at the thought. "Open it," I said. "Just be careful. Get grape juice on it and I'll kill you."

She narrowed her eyes at me, but played along. She pulled the box toward her and lifted the lid. Her mouth fell open and she looked over at me, excitement sparkling in her bright blue eyes. "Is this what I think it is?"

I nodded. "Can you believe she gave it to me?"

"Take it out. I want to see," she said.

I lifted the wedding veil from the box and placed the tiara on my head, pushing the cathedral-length lace veil behind me. I stood up and turned so she could see the pearls woven into the delicate fabric. "Isn't it gorgeous?"

"Wow," she said. "It's perfect. I mean, for a white veil, I guess. When I get married, I'm going to wear all black."

I giggled and reached up to remove it when the back door opened.

Lea stepped halfway inside, and then froze.

Her face turned to stone, and when our eyes met, my stomach twisted. Dammit. The smile faded from my lips and I dropped my eyes to my feet.

"Sorry, we were just—"

"Forget it," she muttered.

I turned and wrapped the lace around the tiara and placed it back inside the box. I couldn't get that look on her face out of my mind. I hated knowing something that brought me so much joy could bring an equal amount of pain to someone else.

It was going to be awkward around here for a while, and I made a mental note to be a lot more careful about making any references to the wedding here in the main rooms of the house.

I closed the top of the box and placed it back inside my bag so she didn't have to look at it.

"We missed you at school today, by the way," I said.

The muscles in Lea's jaw tightened and she took a deep breath. Without a single word, she blew past me and disappeared into the hallway.

I dropped my shoulders and ran a hand over my forehead. "Man, that sucked."

"The veil is beautiful," Mary Anne said. "You shouldn't let her keep you from enjoying this."

"I feel like an asshole," I said, slumping back down in my chair. "How am I going to plan an entire wedding with us both living in the same house? I feel like I'm torturing her."

"She'll get over it," Mary Anne said with a shrug. "You have to live your life."

"Put yourself in her position," I said. I touched the satin edge of the box peeking out of the bag and shook my head. "I never meant to hurt her."

"You have the biggest heart of anyone I've ever met, " Mary Anne said. "If she doesn't know that, that's on her."

"I'm going to put this away for now." I stood and lifted the backpack onto my shoulder.

The back door opened again, and I spun around, expecting to see another one of my friends. Instead, Tuli, my handmaiden from the castle, stood in the doorway, her face pale and full of fear. She could barely catch her breath.

Fear gripped me, and I dropped the bag to the floor.

"Tuli, what is it?" I asked. All I could see in my mind were the drawings Jackson had shown me of my father's domed city in the Southern Kingdom, the streets running with blood.

"Hunters," she said between breaths. "We need help."

I ran into the hallway, my heart beating wildly. "Lea," I shouted. She was making her way up the stairs, but stopped and turned, her eyes wide. "Grab anyone who's still here. My father's castle is being attacked."

Mary Anne ran past me and up the stairs, calling for Essex. Jackson and Aerden came to stand on the landing above the staircase. My eyes met Jackson's across the distance.

"It's happening," I said.

I shifted to white smoke, taking my faster demon form and flying through the hall and out the back door. I reached the lake in seconds.

White roses covered the banks of the small lake, their perfect blooms still bright even in the nearly freezing November air. I stepped among the flowers and let my body pass from the human world to the Shadow World, knowing this was what we had been waiting for. This is what we'd been afraid of for months.

The war with the Order of Shadows had finally found us again.

Out Of Time

Harper

I stepped through the portal and entered a war zone.

Magic of every type collided with the invisible dome that protected the city, going off like multi-colored fireworks, blossoming as sparks flew in every direction. The dome absorbed the attacks, but I knew the magic wouldn't hold forever.

Above the madness of color and explosions, dark shadowy figures flew past like ghosts, their rotting faces illuminated with each of the blasts.

Hunters.

More of them than I'd ever seen or imagined.

My heart tightened, and I had to force back the wild feeling of panic that threatened to unravel me.

A group of guards had gathered on the steps of my father's castle, and I quickly shifted and flew toward them. The head of the guards, Gregory, my father's most trusted second-in-command, grabbed my arm when I shifted back to my human form.

"Princess, thank God you're here," he said. "I've got two dozen of my best soldiers out there, but the hunters have already managed to bring down the first two layers of the shield."

My breath caught in my throat, and I swallowed back my terror. "Two gone already? How long have they been here?"

"Only ten minutes at most," he said. "What do you want us to do?"

My entire body shook with tension. The hunters had brought down two of our five shields in just ten minutes? It had taken us months to build those shields. At this rate, they would break through in a matter of minutes.

I couldn't let that happen. The entire population of the Southern Kingdom lived inside this dome. If the hunters broke through, it would be a catastrophe.

I tried not to think of Jackson's drawings. The rivers of blood running through these streets. I knew his visions always came true, but I also knew how often we had misinterpreted them.

If I believed that was our fate, there would be no reason to fight. No hope of survival. And no matter what, we could not lose hope.

I looked up at the sky, now covered with soldiers and hunters locked in combat above.

"How many are there?" I asked. "I didn't think there were so many hunters in the entire kingdom. It looks like a hundred or more. How can that be?"

Gregory shook his head. "I don't know, Your Highness. We need a plan."

As he stared at me, I suddenly realized he was waiting for me to take control. He expected me to come up with a plan that would save us all.

I closed my eyes and forced back the fears that threatened to overwhelm me. In the months since my father died, I'd never been challenged as a leader here in the Southern Kingdom. Other than settling a few disputes here and there and working to fortify the shields and barriers, the domed city had pretty much run itself.

Angela and I shared the duties, neither of us ready to step into our father's shoes.

I sure as hell wasn't ready for this. How could I possibly save us all? What could I do?

But there was no time for self-doubt and worry. They were waiting for me to give commands, and we were running out of time.

I opened my eyes and took a deep breath.

"We need to get the children to safety," I said. "Send five guards door to door. Have them gather the children and anyone else who is unable to defend themselves. Take them down to the castle's training rooms and have them barricade the doors."

Gregory chose five of the nearest guards and passed on my orders. I turned and studied the streets of the town. Many of the citizens had come out of their houses and were just standing there, staring at the chaos above, complete and total terror locking them in place.

"I need you to send another two guards out into the city to round up anyone who is able to fight," I said. "We may only have ten or twenty minutes at best before the hunters break through the dome. When they come through, I want everyone who can carry a weapon or cast magic to be assembled here on the castle steps and inside the throne room. Have some of the guards fortify the balconies and other entrances to the castle. Do whatever it takes to make sure the only way inside is through this main door."

"What about the guards up there with the hunters? Should we send more through?"

I looked at the group assembled on the steps of the castle. Was it better to send them out to try and take the hunters down? Or protect the castle and the children?

All I could do was go with my gut instinct, which told me to send them out to fight. If we could turn the tide and take a few of the hunters down, maybe it would slow their progress in taking down the magical barriers that protected the rest of the city.

"Send half of the guards who are left out to fight with the rest," I said. "The other half stays here on the steps as the first wave of defense. Place the villagers behind them in rows leading up to the castle."

As he gave the command, my friends from Peachville ran across the garden to join me on the steps. Jackson, Aerden, Mary Anne, Essex, Lea, Courtney, and Zara. Nearly everyone and everything in

61

the world that mattered to me was now protected by a thin, invisible barrier that could fall in less than half an hour.

Jackson grabbed my hand. "What can we do? What's the plan?"

"The guards are getting the children to safety," I said. "Mary Anne and Courtney, since you can't cast human magic here inside the dome, I need you to go help them round up the children and the elderly or disabled and take them into the castle. Try to help keep them calm. And Courtney?"

She turned toward me, pushing her dark blonde hair behind her ears. Her eyes were wide and filled with such fear, it broke my heart.

"When you get downstairs, I need you to meditate and save your strength. If the hunters break through, I may send for you. Your ability to recharge magic could save us all."

She nodded quickly and then lowered her gaze to the ground. She was such a sweet soul. So shy and reserved, but so incredibly powerful. When a witch had spent all her power and was beyond exhaustion, Courtney could completely refill her energy in a matter of minutes.

It was a rare gift, and one that we may desperately need before the night was over.

Mary Anne and Essex held each other for a long moment, and then separated. The two girls disappeared through the crowd of citizens gathering near the castle steps.

"We need to get out there," I said. "They've already gotten through two of our shields, and the rest won't hold much longer. If we can't reduce their numbers, it's going to be a bloodbath once they break through. There's just too many of them."

"I've never seen so many hunters," Lea said. "The Order must have been creating new ones. There's no way this many existed last time we were here in the Shadow World."

"We should have been patrolling the land more," I said. "Maybe we would have seen what was going on."

"You can't worry about that now," Jackson said.

Lea pushed past me. "I'm going out there," she said. "I've been waiting for a good chance to kick some hunter ass."

She shifted to black smoke. Aerden followed her, the two of them disappearing into the crowd of citizens gathered in the square outside the castle's entrance.

"Jackson, I need you and Essex to get up there and see if you can figure out how they're getting through the shields. Last time they used some kind of liquid, but I don't see anything like that this time."

I looked around until I saw a young guard standing on the stairs. I called him over. "Marcus, right?"

He nodded, swallowing hard and straightening his shoulders. "Yes, Princess."

"Follow these two demons into battle overhead. Stay by their side, and if they figure out what the hunters are using to get through our shields, come down here immediately and let me know."

He sucked in a breath and gave me a salute.

My stomach turned and tightened. How had my life come to this? Was I really someone guards saluted? I didn't feel at all ready for this kind of responsibility. I needed my sister here.

"Zara," I said. "Can you go back through the portal and get Angela for me? Call her first and make sure she's home and then get her over here as fast as possible."

Zara looked up at the explosions still crashing above our heads and nodded. "I'll be back as soon as I can," she said. She started to go, but looked up once more and paused. She turned back toward Jackson. "There's something weird about those clusters of hunters closest to the dome. I can't put my finger on it, but they don't look right."

He nodded and looked up. "We need to get out there and get a closer look."

My eyes threatened to fill with hot tears, the sides stinging. I blinked several times and waited for Jackson's eyes to meet mine. I hated being separated from him. I hated staying down here while he went up to battle, but it was my duty to stay with my people. They needed me here, where I could direct the rest of the army.

But I knew the moment he left the safety of the dome, it would be too dark and too chaotic above to track him and know that he was okay.

"Be careful," I said. I threw my arms around him and held him to me. "I love you."

"I love you, too," he said. He glanced at Essex and the two of them shifted and flew through the streets toward the only exit out of the dome.

Gregory appeared at my side again. "I've just had a report from one of my men. The third shield has gone down, Your Highness."

I looked up at the dome again, horrified by the number of bodies that now littered the curve of the domed surface. It was hard to see from here, but it didn't look as if the hunters' numbers had been thinned at all. I counted at least six of my guards now limp and unmoving against the barrier.

"I need you to find the demon girl who created our shields," I said. "Willow. She should be inside, heading toward the dungeons, possibly. Have her brought back up and see if she can do something to help fortify the primary shield."

"Yes, Princess," he said with a crisp salute. He turned to two guards at his side and sent them flying into the castle to find Willow.

I looked around. Everyone hurried to get inside the castle or to line up on the castle steps, weapons in hand. The fight raged above, our defenses growing weaker by the second.

I stood in the middle of the action, feeling totally helpless. I longed to be outside in the fight, making a difference. Was Jackson okay? Had any of the hunters been killed?

I could barely make out what was happening through all the smoke and darkness above.

I climbed the steps of the castle, deciding to move closer to the top of the dome so I could get a better view of the battlefield above us. Impatient, I shifted into white smoke and flew over the steps, through the throne room, and out onto the small balcony that overlooked the city.

I leaned against the white stone railing and let my eyes sweep across the top of the dome.

A small group of guards were clustered around a hunter just above where I stood, but even though they were fighting with every weapon and skill available to them, they didn't seem to be doing any damage to the hunters. In fact, the hunters weren't fighting back at all. Spells seemed to bounce off them, as if my guards were nothing more than an annoyance.

I watched as two guards threw spears made of ice directly toward the hunter's heart. My mouth fell open as the ice disintegrated into nothing a few seconds before they made contact with her. She hadn't even lifted a hand against their spells, so how had she managed to deflect their magic?

It was almost as if the hunter had been cloaked in a shield of her own. Something impenetrable to the magic of the guards.

My stomach knotted in fear. There was no hope of defending ourselves against an invincible foe. What were we missing?

I shifted again and flew back down to the bottom steps of the castle's entrance. Gregory met me there, Willow at his side.

The young demon curtsied and lowered her head. "Princess."

I placed my palm beneath her chin and raised her eyes to mine. "Willow, is there anything you can do to keep the primary shield up if the secondary one goes down?"

"I can try," she said. "But the most I can do against this many attacks coming through all at once is buy us a few minutes."

A loud boom echoed through the streets of the dome and everyone around me ducked, our eyes lifting toward the sky to see what could have caused such a noise. A deep blue light shimmered across the surface of the dome and then disappeared.

"Oh my God," Willow whispered beside me.

"What?" I asked, panic gripping my heart. "What was that?"

Her face grew pale and she stared at me with wide, green eyes. "The secondary shield just went down."

Sarra Cannon

Bring It

Lea

Hunters were everywhere.

I had never seen a group of them so organized and so damned hard to kill. I took my demon form and flew high into the trees on the north side of the domed city, settling on a limb before I retook solid form. I stayed out of sight, knowing my best advantage in this fight was my skill with the bow. From here, I could take out a dozen of these things before they even knew what hit them.

I nocked a mystical arrow and took aim. I closed one eye and steadied myself, choosing a target low on the field of battle. Before I let the arrow fly, though, I surveyed the area around her, picking out half a dozen, studying their exact locations and calculating their positions. If I acted fast, I could take all six out in a matter of seconds.

I took a deep breath, and as I exhaled, I let the first arrow fly. I didn't pause to see if my arrow had met its mark. Instead, I moved to the next target, conjuring a second arrow. In seconds, I had sent six arrows soaring through the air. One by one, they each hit their marks.

Or did they?

The hunters seemed completely unaffected, even though I knew my aim had been true. I prepared another arrow, watching more closely this time as I took aim and sent it soaring toward its mark.

As I suspected, a tiny shimmer of light pulsed around the hunter's body as the arrow disintegrated on contact.

They were shielded.

I narrowed my gaze and pressed my lips into a tight smile. Let's see if they can shield against these.

I focused my energy on conjuring a special type of arrow I'd been working on. Man, I'd been dying to see what these babies could do in a real battle. My pulse pounded in my ears as I nocked the first of my shield-piercing arrows. It took more of my mental focus and physical energy to create these, but if this worked, it was worth it.

I watched as each of my new arrows flew through the air, sinking deep into all six of the hunters' hearts in rapid succession.

I expected them to clutch their hearts and collapse onto the domed shield beneath them. Instead, they disintegrated into a puff of dust that fell on the shield and slid down to nothingness. I straightened my shoulders and widened my eyes.

Something was not right about this. Dust was not how hunters died. Their physical forms might be rotted and decaying, but they didn't simply turn to dust.

I'd watched many hunters die, and it usually involved a grotesque display of black blood and oozing decayed flesh. I looked across the battlefield, searching for the next closest group of targets. They sent spell after exploding spell toward the shield below them, paying no attention to the armed soldiers rushing toward them.

I steadied myself against the thick support of the tree and nocked another of my piercing arrows. Locating my next six targets, I unleashed another storm of arrows. Again, they met their marks and the hunters turned to dust.

I let my bow fall to my side and waited, watching the battlefield, trying to make sense of what was really going on down there. Shielded hunters made of dust? It didn't make sense.

A nearby shriek caught my attention, and my head snapped toward the sound. A hunter floated in the air about twenty feet above the rest, her head turned in my direction. Her glowing red eyes sought me out, and when she located me in the trees, she opened her mouth again and let out a loud scream that sent the group of soldiers around her flying backward through the air as if she'd physically hit them with the sound.

In an instant, more than two dozen smaller hunters below stopped their barrage of attacks on the dome and turned to me instead. They moved in complete unison, like some eerie chorus of death-dealers.

With a flick of her hand, the hunter above sent the smaller minions toward me. In that instant, it all clicked. The hunters closer to the dome were not actually hunters at all. They were shades— conjured minions bespelled to look and act like hunters, but not nearly as powerful. They'd been shielded to make them seem unstoppable, but once those shields were down, they would be easier to kill than flies.

I smiled and raised an eyebrow as I lifted my bow and conjured three arrows at once.

I'd never practiced fighting two dozen targets at once, but there was no time like the present. And I had some serious aggression to work out. I glanced at the hunter hovering above the others, meeting her eye without fear.

Bring it, I thought as I drew back my bow and let the first set of triple arrows fly.

Sarra Cannon

Broken

Aerden

I couldn't find her.

I had followed Lea through the gate of the dome, but she'd disappeared into the darkness of the forest surrounding the city. I frantically searched the area for any sign of her, but there was no way to know exactly where she'd gone, and I couldn't afford to waste time while everyone else was fighting.

Dammit, why had she gone off on her own like that?

Knowing Lea, she'd wanted to get a bird's-eye view of the battlefield. She'd probably set herself up in the trees somewhere so she could assassinate as many of these things as possible without being seen.

It was a good strategy, but it nearly drove me out of my mind. How could I protect her if I couldn't even find her? I had to hope that meant none of the hunters could find her, either.

"Aerden, let's go," Jackson called as he flew by, Essex at his side. His hands were already covered in an icy-blue glow as he shifted to his solid form and landed near the closest group of hunters.

Jackson touched his palms to the surface of the dome, sending a path of solid ice straight toward the group. When it reached them, the ice encircled their entire group of six and shot straight into the air, encasing them in a thick wall.

From inside their bluish prison, the hunters beat against the walls with their fists and cast fire spells to try to burn their way out. The ice had already begun to melt.

I knew I needed to join the fight, but something deep inside me protested. I pushed against it, raising my hands and preparing to cast magic for the first time since I'd been freed from my slavery.

But I couldn't call up my magic.

Instead, a sudden fever flushed my skin. My head began to throb. I closed my eyes and pressed my hands against my temples.

The face of a witch pushed its way into my mind, her voice so loud in my memory, I couldn't hear the battle raging around me. *"You are mine,"* she said. *"And you will do as I command you."*

I beat my hands against my head and cried out, but I couldn't shake the memories. I fell to my knees against the hard surface of the ground, just wanting it to stop.

I'd rushed out here, blindly following Lea and thinking only of her safety, but now, I realized why I'd refused to participate in the training. Why I'd always insisted on using physical weapons when Lea and I sparred.

"Your magic belongs to me, demon," the voice in my head reminded me.

"No," I shouted into the night air. "Not anymore. I don't answer to you anymore."

I tried to stand, but my knees were too weak.

What the hell was wrong with me? I was free. I was no longer bound to any witch in the Order. I didn't have to answer to anyone but myself.

I managed to find my footing and draw the strength to stand, but the fear of casting left me trembling. The horror of my reality struck me so hard, I nearly fell again.

I had lived for so long with no free will, only able to use my magic when the witch I was bound to commanded it or needed my protection, that now, even though I was free, I was too broken to summon my powers without someone here to control me.

My lips trembled, and I clenched my teeth so hard my jaw hurt. I breathed in and out, panic flowing through me like air.

What had become of me?

I used to be a warrior. I used to be strong.

The past few months, I'd told myself I wasn't casting magic because I wanted to stretch my limbs and feel the cold steel of a sword against my skin or the rough wood of a staff in my grip. But I'd been a fool.

I hadn't used magic because I was powerless. Too broken by years of slavery to access my strength without a master's voice in my head telling me what to do.

I lifted my eyes to the battle above, knowing there was a time when I could have made a difference. When I could have fought alongside my brother and seen terror in the eyes of my foes as I unleashed my fury upon them.

Instead, here I stood, paralyzed like that statue I'd been bound to for years while the Order searched for the missing Peachville Prima. Sixteen long years encased in stone, unable to cast or speak or feel anything but the hard, unyielding pressure of the stone against my form.

A dark shadow raced toward me and my brother materialized, out of breath, his face flush from battle. "Aerden, we need you," he said. "These hunters are using some type of shield. We need every demon fighting. What are you doing down here?"

I shook my head slowly, afraid to meet his eyes. I didn't want him to see what I'd become. I didn't want him to know how weak I was. Not when I used to be the stronger one. I couldn't face it.

Jackson stepped toward me and placed a hand on my arm. I pulled away from him, but he moved with me, gripping my chin with his fingers and forcing my eyes to his.

He studied me, and for a moment, I felt see-through. My sorrows were laid bare in excruciating detail before him, my soul in agony.

His features softened and his eyes grew wider.

"Here," he said, pulling a dagger from his belt. He released my chin and flipped the dagger over, handing it to me. "You don't have to cast. Just kill as many of those bastards as you can with this. Think of it as your first shot at payback. One for every year those evil bitches took away from you."

Over the past few months, I'd pushed my brother away. I'd blamed him for Lea's unhappiness, all the while avoiding my own. He'd nagged me to talk about what happened, and how many times had I told him to leave me alone? How many times had I told him I was fine and that he couldn't possibly understand?

But there in his eyes, I saw for the first time that he understood a lot more than I gave him credit for.

I wrapped my hand around the hilt of the dagger, surprised by the confidence that surged through me at the feel of demon steel against my skin.

I nodded, and then looked up again toward the battlefield surrounding the domed city.

Maybe I was strong enough, after all.

The Hunter's Heart

Lea

My arrows downed more than half of the shades rushing toward me, but there were ten still standing by the time they got too close for my arrows to have any hope of destroying them. Besides, conjuring the piercing arrows was taking more out of me than I anticipated.

As the first of their group reached my perch on the tree limb, I quickly shifted to smoke, hooking my bow over my shoulder as I moved and launching myself upward. I flew straight over the group and reformed at the edge of the limb, reaching for the two swords at my side.

My blades struck the shields around the shades and recoiled back toward me.

If they had been able to react faster, I would have been in some serious trouble, but I had the element of surprise on my side. They hadn't expected me to reappear behind them, and they'd built up far too much momentum on their flight toward me to turn and face me fast enough.

I guess their master wasn't used to managing so many puppets at once.

With their shields up, though, I wasn't going to be able to damage them at such a close range. I had two choices. I could either try to get far enough away to conjure more piercing arrows and kill a few more shades, or I could go after the hunter herself.

I chose the hunter, hoping that if I could bring her down, her remaining shades would disappear.

I jumped on the far end of the limb, using it as a springboard to send me flying through the air. I somersaulted backward, crossing my blades in front of my chest as I reached the hunter just a few feet behind me.

She was much faster to react than her minions had been. Even though my swords slashed through the front of her robes and tore away some of her decaying flesh, I hadn't landed a significant blow.

A white-hot pain sliced across my right arm as I descended, and I cried out. The surprise of the attack unbalanced me, but I managed to shift before the hunter was able to cut straight through my arm.

I flew higher into the trees, reforming on a thin limb toward the very top. I backed against the trunk and sheathed my two swords. I ripped a long strip of fabric from the bottom of my shirt and, using my teeth to help pull it taut, fashioned a tourniquet on my upper arm to stop the rush of blood from my wound.

I reached for my bow and tried to nock an arrow, thinking I could at least bring down a few more shades at this distance before they realized where I'd gone, but my arm protested, refusing to pull back on the string. The silver blade of the hunter's dagger had sliced clean through my muscle. My bow would be no use to me right now.

I clenched my teeth against the pain and rage and stared down at the rotting hunter. She was going to pay for that.

With my uninjured left arm, I unsheathed one of my swords and jumped down toward her. She screeched and lifted her arms as I attacked, but instead of slicing her to shreds like it should have done, my blade collided with an invisible shield around the hunter's body. The shades who had remained nearby all turned to dust, tiny fragments shimmering as their magic dissipated, the power returned to the hunter herself.

She must have anticipated my attack and recalled her power, shifting the magic she'd been using to shield her minions to protect herself. She smiled with what was left of her lips and pushed me backward with a bony hand. I stumbled and fell from the tree, my body nearly hitting the ground before I was able to shift to smoke and fly back up toward her.

I reformed on a sturdier limb and quickly placed my blade back in its sheath at my hip.

How the hell was I going to hurt her if she had a shield around her? Now that I knew what to look for, I could see the slight shimmer of it wavering around her. I had a feeling it was a more powerful form of magical protection than any I'd encountered on a hunter in the past.

Someone had planned this attack with precision. Someone who knew how powerful we were when tested.

Between my injured dominant arm and the uselessness of my blade, I knew there was nothing I could do to defeat her out here by myself.

Shit. I hated to walk away from a fight, but I wasn't an idiot. Unless I could figure out a way to destroy that shield, there was no hope of killing her.

She lurched toward me, but I shifted and flew back toward the dome, the hunter close at my heels.

I reformed among a group of soldiers fighting on the surface of what remained of the dome. Their magic and weapons had done little to challenge the minions they were fighting.

"These hunters aren't real," I shouted over the sound of explosions and the clash of steel. "They're conjured by the larger hunters hovering above. Concentrate all your attacks on them. Spread the word."

"How do we get through their shields?" the soldier closest to me shouted. A wound across his forehead poured blood into his eyes, but I respected the fact that he merely swiped at it and kept fighting.

"They seem to be powerful, but I doubt the shields are permanent," I said. I searched the skies above the dome for the hunter who had attacked me, but there was no sign of her. Something twisted in my gut.

I doubt she had given up, and now that I'd lost sight of her, she could be anywhere.

"They've nearly broken through the dome," another soldier shouted from a few feet away. "Only the primary barrier remains."

Panic flashed across the faces of all around me. It was everyone's worst nightmare, and I knew that if we didn't get these hunters down fast, the entire city would fall.

"Get everyone who's out here to concentrate all their forces on those larger hunters," I shouted. "Bring their shields down and these shades should fall."

I rushed along the surface of the dome, directing soldiers to focus their attacks on the hunters floating above when something in the trees to my left caught my eye. Movement, and the shimmer of something as it caught the light of a passing bolt of lightning.

I paused and searched the treeline, excitement pumping through my veins.

Then I saw her.

Another hunter, hiding among the shadows just inside the thick forest. Her glowing red eyes were locked on the dome's surface, her hands moving in circles as she maintained some type of powerful spell.

I glanced back at the others, wondering if I should grab a few of them to help. I scanned the field of battle, searching for any sign of my demon friends.

But I was running out of time. The dome would collapse before we had a chance to save it if I didn't act now.

The city's guards were making progress with the hunters above the battlefield, and several of their shields had gone down, but if my suspicions were correct, that solo hunter in the shadows was the one attacking the dome.

If I could bring her down or break her concentration, Harper and the others inside the dome might have a chance.

I shifted and flew around the other side of the trees, sneaking up behind the hunter, praying I still had the element of surprise on my side.

When I took my solid form on a sturdy limb about twenty feet behind her, I waited, barely breathing. When I was sure she hadn't noticed me, I slowly reached for my bow. As quietly as I could, I conjured a set of three piercing arrows and took a deep breath.

This was going to hurt like a bitch.

Pain shot through my arm like fire, and I had to slowly release my pull. I bit down on my lip, fighting against the pain. With this damned wound, there was no way I would be able to pull the arrows back enough to hit my target accurately.

But then, I caught a brief glimpse of Aerden down below on the battleground of the dome. He sliced through the hunters' shades with ease, not even using his magic to bring them down. I smiled at the thought of how often he'd insisted I train with my non-dominant arm. I'd been annoyed at the time, but now, I realized he might have just saved us all.

I switched my bow to my right hand and nocked the three arrows, pulling the string back with my stronger, uninjured left hand. I should have practiced more, but I prayed it would be enough. Just this once.

I inhaled, and then with a slow and steady exhale, I released the arrows, aiming straight for the hunter's heart.

Sarra Cannon

I Knew Her

Jackson

The battlefield above the dome was pure chaos. Aerden was having more luck breaking through the shields that protected the hunters than anyone. He powered through the shields, bringing them down and slicing through the hunters. But there were too many of them.

Essex and I battled our way through the masses of attackers, searching for any true signs of the real source of their power.

There was no way these simple fireballs and poison bolts were breaking down the barrier this quickly. It would take a force ten times this to take down a single piece of the dome's outer shield, much less break through to the last remaining barrier in half an hour. What were we missing?

Were these hunters just a diversion?

I pushed through to a clear spot on the edge of the throng and shifted, flying higher to get a better view of the entire area. There was a definite hierarchy at play here. The hunters near the dome were concentrated in groups of six, clustered together and each of them casting the exact same spell over and over. Above the large group, about ten taller hunters seemed to be casting spells of their own, but I couldn't see what magic they were using.

They weren't directly attacking the dome, so what were they doing?

My eye caught a group of guards soaring up toward one of these larger hunters, concentrating all their attacks on her, instead. I narrowed my eyes, studying the battlefield as guards on the surface rushed from group to group. Whatever message they were spreading, someone had obviously told them to focus on the larger hunters.

In seconds, I understood why. As a group on the far side of the dome broke through a protective shield around the large hunter, the smaller ones below her froze and then turned to dust that shimmered slightly as it fell across the invisible shield.

Holy crap. Those had not been real hunters at all. They were conjured minions. It all made sense now how they had managed to create such incredible numbers in such a short period of time. They weren't real.

If we could break through and bring down the remaining nine hunters, we could save the city after all.

But if those hunters had been concentrating on directing the attacks of their conjured armies, what magic was bringing down the shields?

I searched again, frantic to figure this out before it was too late.

Harper was right. The last time hunters had successfully brought down the city's dome, they had used a corrosive liquid that ate through the defenses. This time, I couldn't see anyone using liquid or a spell that would have been strong enough to bring down those shields.

That's when a dark braid caught my eye.

Lea.

She had noticed something in the treeline and shifted, disappearing into the forest surrounding the city.

I flew down toward the young guard Harper had sent out with us. "Marcus, I need you to go back inside the city and tell Harper that the dozens of hunters attacking the shield aren't real. They're shades, conjured by the real hunters floating above them," I said. "Tell her to send anyone out here who has magic that can penetrate personal shields. They need to go after those nine or ten hovering above the rest."

The guard nodded and shifted to white smoke—the color of those demons native to the Southern Kingdom.

I looked toward the area where I had last seen Lea and shifted to black shadow—the color of my own people from the north.

I flew up toward her, careful to stay among the shadows in case a more dangerous army lay in wait here in the trees. Now that I was high above the battlefield, the shouts and explosions were farther away. I listened, my eyes scanning the trees for any sign of her.

At first, I couldn't make out anything unusual. I had the unique ability to see in the dark, so it should have been easy for me to make out any kind of secret army or group of witches hiding out back here, away from view.

I doubled back toward the battlefield and came through the forest from another angle, hoping to find where Lea had gone.

It took mere seconds to locate her, about fifty yards away, tucked close to a tree, her feet planted firmly on a thick limb about midway up a large tree. She raised her bow and winced as she attempted to pull it back for an attack.

That's when I noticed the makeshift tourniquet on her right arm. Blood soaked her sleeve. Her bow arm seemed badly injured. My first instinct was to go to her. I wasn't a great healer, but I did have some ability to cure wounds.

But I hesitated, my eyes following her own gaze toward something hovering in the trees between us.

A hunter. And one I recognized.

Mayor Chen, the former mayor of Peachville. She had secretly been one of Priestess Winter's own daughters from a previous generation. A second, sent in with a disguise to gain trust and keep an eye on the coven. I knew she'd survived the battle against

Priestess Winter, but she disappeared soon after.

Someone had done this to her, draining her life and turning her into this rotting thing.

Half of the mayor's face was missing completely, the bones showing through what was left of her shredded and decayed skin. But I knew her.

It hit me hard, seeing what had become of her. She'd fought on the wrong side of our war, so why had she been punished like this? Was it because she'd failed to protect her priestess?

Was she the one orchestrating all of this? Who had sent her?

Lea switched to her off-hand and winced as she pulled back on the string of her bow, three conjured arrows set to fly. She let them go, and I watched as they flew through the air, their silvery tips shining through the darkness toward their mark.

At that exact moment, an explosion rocked the battlefield. Shouts rang out, and a bright light flashed. The hunter moved, Lea's arrows missing her by a fraction of an inch. Her eyes were on the battlefield, a gruesome smile stretching her lips across teeth and bone.

But as one of the arrows grazed the edge of her robes, her head snapped toward Lea.

My head jerked, stuck in this moment between Lea here in the woods and Harper down in the city below, what remained of the hunters and their shades pouring in through a giant crack in the center of the dome's surface.

From where I hovered in the treetops, I could just make out Harper's blonde hair waving like a flag on the castle steps. She was surrounded by guards, but my heart clenched. I wanted to go to her. To protect her.

But I couldn't abandon Lea.

The hunter moved toward her, and without time to formulate a plan, I flew around and shifted to human form between them. I crouched down and touched my icy hands to the tree's limbs, pushing my magic outward from my body so that ice traveled the path from my hands to where the hunter hovered. I lifted my palms upward and the ice rose to encase the hunter's entire body, blue light flickering from inside the magic.

She was frozen, but I knew the ice wouldn't hold her long.

"The dome's been breached," I shouted to Lea. "We have to go. Are you okay? You're hurt."

"It's nothing," she said. "But I can't leave. I think this hunter is the one who's been shielding all of the others, and I think she's the one whose magic just brought down the dome. We have to kill her if the others have any chance of survival."

I glanced back toward the castle. Harper had a sword in her hand and was rushing into the mass of dark hunters and shades. I reminded myself of her strength, but a piece of me could not bear the thought of her fighting without me by her side.

But there was no time to act. The ice around the hunter's body cracked and her bony hands broke through, ripping the ice from around her. She turned her red eyes to us, anger flaring as she prepared to scream.

Sarra Cannon

They Aren't After Me

Harper

An explosion rocked the city. Hunters poured through the crack in the dome's final shield and chaos erupted on the streets below.

I didn't know what to expect, but my greatest fear was that the hunters would head straight for the homes in the main village to steal demons for the Order of Shadows. That's why I had told the guards to hide the children in the rooms below the castle.

But the hunters didn't head for the demons. They headed straight for the castle. Straight for me.

I took human form and planted my feet at the bottom of the steps. I summoned my energy and my arms rose as flames coated my hands. With a flick of my wrists, streams of fire shot toward the group of hunters first to reach me.

Beside me, Gregory conjured spears made of pale shimmering light and hurled them toward the hunters, one at a time. A few of the spears flew straight into the hearts of the smaller hunters and their bodies disintegrated into dust.

Confused, I watched as the hunters fell way too easily. What was going on?

"Shades," Marcus shouted as he approached through the wave of attackers.

"What does that mean?" I asked. "They aren't real hunters?"

"Not all of them," he said. "Jackson sent me to find you. He said it looks like most of them are just conjured mirrors of the hunters. The real ones have been protecting them, but it looks like they are vulnerable, now. Aim for their hearts."

Jackson was alive. "Where is he?"

"He was still outside, fighting the larger hunters," he said.

I took a deep breath and turned to focus on the fight at hand. Jackson was a skilled warrior, and he was out there with Lea and Aerden and Essex. They could handle themselves, but I hated that I couldn't see him.

Still, everyone was counting on me to lead them, and we were under some serious fire.

"Princess, we need to get you inside to safety," Gregory said, grabbing my arm.

I pulled away. I had already stayed out of the fight long enough. It was my duty to protect this castle and the children hiding inside. I wouldn't back down while everyone else risked their lives.

"I'm staying," I said, meeting his eyes so he knew there was no use arguing with me. "Concentrate our forces on the real hunters. We can't let them inside the castle."

I shifted and flew toward the entrance to the castle's throne room and grabbed a long sword from a pile of weapons the guards had collected from my father's training rooms below. I turned my eyes toward the approaching hunters.

With lightning-fast movements, I shifted back and forth between my two forms, sword flying as I fought my way through the lesser shades toward the real hunters.

By now, many of the guards had realized what was going on and had come up on the backs of the hunters, surrounding them. In minutes, the smaller shades had all been destroyed, leaving us with five real hunters left to kill.

I took a deep breath as they approached, their mouths open and ready to scream.

I didn't want to wait for the first one to reach me. Instead, I shifted, gathering speed in the air as I reformed and aimed my sword at the heart inside her rotting flesh.

Only, the sword could not penetrate her shield.

The force of the impact twisted the weapon from my hand and it fell to the stone street with a loud clang.

Spells soared through the air as all our forces threw every ounce of power toward the hunters. But nothing seemed to damage them. I expected the hunter standing above me to attack, so I left my sword where it lay and shifted quickly to move out of her way. I expected her to search the crowd for me and move in for her attack, but she didn't.

Instead, she set her eyes on my father's castle and floated up the steps at terrible speeds.

They aren't after me.

"Don't let them reach the castle," I shouted to anyone who could hear me over the sounds of battle. I had no idea what it was they wanted from inside. The children? I wasn't sure, but whatever it was, it was important enough to send a massive, coordinated attack against our city. Which meant it was extremely important for me to make sure they never got inside.

"Gregory," I shouted as I ran back toward my sword and retrieved it from the street.

His head turned toward me, but his arms were raised, pushing a hunter back with all his strength.

"Do whatever you have to do to keep them out here," I said.

"Where are you going?" he asked.

I nodded toward the castle. "I'm going after that one."

I shifted, sword in hand, and flew up the steps toward the hunter. She had almost reached the entrance to the throne room. I knew I wouldn't be able to kill her with her shield still in place, but as far as I knew, hunters couldn't pass through solid objects. I just had to find a way to hold her back.

I flew past the hunter and reformed in the doorway just in front of her. I dropped the sword onto the steps and flattened my palms toward the stones below. I cursed the wide entrance to the castle. This wasn't going to be easy and it was going to cause some real damage, but I had no other choice.

I exhaled and pushed my power deep down in the stones at my feet. With my mind, I wrapped my energy around those stones and lifted my hands, pulling them with me. A wall of rock rose from the ground, covering half of the main entrance with more than a foot of solid stone.

I stumbled back and took a deep breath.

The hunter was almost to the entrance, and there was still enough of an opening at the top for her to pass through. I knew I wouldn't be able to raise the floor any higher, but there was just as much stone above the entrance as below. I pushed my palms out toward my side and ropes of white smoke formed.

I whipped the ropes up toward the balcony, wrapping the smoky coils around the stone banister. With all my strength, I pulled downward. The balcony collapsed on top of the stone barrier I'd built, covering what remained of the entrance and blocking the hunter from going inside.

She reached the top of the steps just as the last of the stones settled into place. Her skeletal hands circled my wrists and yanked me backward, breaking my concentration. But the damage was already done. If she wanted inside the castle, she was going to have to find another way in. I prayed the guards had done a good job of sealing all the balconies and windows.

The hunter's long green fingernails raked across the skin at my wrists, drawing blood. I twisted and pulled away from her grasp, but when I tried to shift, I stumbled, my vision blurring. I fell against the stones at the entrance and blinked my eyes.

My vision didn't clear. I closed them harder and reopened them, swiping at my eyes, but my movements lagged behind my intentions. I opened my mouth to speak, but all I heard was the sound of the hunter's laughter.

I stared down at my bloodied wrists. She'd poisoned me. I could feel it snaking its way through my bloodstream like a virus, hot and sticky and dark.

I struggled against it, but there was nothing I could do. I collapsed against the stone barrier, unable to lift my arms or move my feet. Everything around me slowed to a crawl, the sounds of battle no longer in my ears. All I could hear was the slowing beat of my heart as my body began to shut down.

The hunter descended on me, and the flash of a dagger caught my blurred vision as she removed it from beneath her ropes and brought it to my neck.

I wanted to cry out for the guards, but my tongue wouldn't work. I had never felt more helpless in my life.

On instinct, I struggled to bring my hands to my throat, to shield myself from the blade. They only jerked and slowly moved up my thigh, and then froze. I couldn't move them an inch farther. The poison worked fast.

The hunter leaned in, preparing to slice my throat, but something about the movement of my hand made her stop. Her head jerked downward and even with my poor vision, I saw the red in her eyes flash bright in recognition.

She removed the blade from my neck and took my hand in hers, instead. She touched my skin almost lovingly. Reverently. The edge of one long fingernail scraped across the top of my sapphire ring, as if she were petting it.

My stomach lurched, and I tried to pull my hand away from her. I wore this ring to keep it safe. To keep it out of the hands of the Order of Shadows. I'd rather die than see them get it back.

I had no idea what use it might be to them now, since the sapphire gates had been destroyed, but I didn't want to take any chances. I had earned that ring, and as the life drained from me, I no longer had the strength to protect it.

The cold steel tip of her dagger pressed against the base of my finger, just below the curve of the ring. The hunter smiled as she pushed the blade into my flesh.

Sarra Cannon

Go To Her

Lea

The hunter rushed toward us. Her red eyes grew wide and her mouth opened in a horrific scream that echoed off the trees and knocked me to my knees. I fell against the limb and covered my ears. I had heard the screams of many hunters over the years, and I knew the force they were capable of, but not once had I ever been downed by one of those screams.

I struggled to stand and lift my bow, but the sound pierced my skull and made my muscles tense and weak.

Jackson pulled me up and wrapped my arm around his shoulders. He shifted and flew backward into the darkness beyond the dome, keeping to the forest shadows. He looped around and brought us back to another set of trees closer to the main city.

He settled me against the trunk of the tree.

"Are you okay?" he asked, out of breath and glancing back toward the castle.

I followed his gaze to where Harper stood, sword in hand.

My heart ached. I had become so used to turning my sadness into anger, but maybe the injury and exhaustion had weakened me. Tears threatened to fall.

Jackson was honorable and would never leave me alone in battle, but his heart was with her. And in that moment, as he stared toward her with such fear and love in his eyes, I realized that it was truly over for us.

Even with the engagement, I don't think I'd really come to terms with it. Not like this.

I turned my head to the side and wiped a tear from my eyes, swearing that would be the last. I would not let this make me weak. I would rather die than let a broken heart destroy me.

"Go to her," I said.

He shook his head, his eyebrows pressed together. "No, I won't leave you," he said. "Let's just catch our breath and take care of that hunter together."

But then he stood, gasping. He took two steps forward and brought a hand to his mouth.

I forced myself to stand, and when I looked toward the castle steps, I saw her. A hunter had forced Harper to the ground, a dagger pressed to her neck.

"Jackson, go," I said more forcefully.

"You'll be okay?" he asked, but he was already moving.

"I can handle myself," I said, pulling my sword from my belt.

He swallowed and nodded, our eyes meeting as he glanced over his shoulder at me. "Thank you," he said, and disappeared.

I took several deep breaths, pushing against the flood of emotions that consumed me. Anger. Loss. Aching regret.

I focused on the anger, drinking it down. I forced my thoughts to the Order and how they had taken so much away from me. From all of us. I channeled those thoughts toward this one hunter still out here in the woods with me.

That bitch was going down.

I straightened my shoulders and looked up toward the trees, trying to locate her in the darkness. But I didn't have to search. She had found me first.

Before I could shift or move or think, the hunter was on me, her long bony fingers devoid of any flesh as they wrapped around my arm. She dug one gnarled fingernail into the wound on my arm, and

I cried out, the pain so great it resonated through every inch of my body.

It was impossible to shift to demon form when such pain gripped me. None of the training I'd done over the past one hundred years had prepared me for the power of that pain. I was helpless against it, a feeling I loathed more than any other.

I pushed against it, like fighting through a deep fog. Somehow, I managed to place my uninjured hand on my sword, but before I could draw it and sink the blade into her decaying frame, she pushed me backward with such force, bones cracked as I hit the trunk of the mighty tree behind me.

I fell against the ground like a ragdoll, and as I lifted my head, I saw a streak of white light rushing toward me. A spell that should have ended me with its power.

I braced myself for the blow, crying out as I realized this could be the last moment of my immortal life.

But the impact never came. Instead, something burned white-hot against the flesh between my breasts.

The key.

It seared my skin, and without thinking, I clawed at the rope that held it around my neck and pulled it away from my flesh, bringing the key outside my shirt.

The diamond gemstone at its center glowed with a faint light and the moment it reached the air, it connected with the residue of the hunter's spell, solidifying it in midair, like water freezing.

When magic was cast here in the Shadow World, it left an invisible trail, able to be seen and followed by those who had the special gift of tracking, but I had never seen a trail solidify like this.

It crystallized, a faint white mist lifting from it as it snaked from the key to the hunter. It all happened so quickly, I could hardly make sense of it.

Her head jerked backward in surprise. She prepared another attack, but I took full advantage of whatever miracle had just saved my life. I pushed up against the tree and forced myself to a standing position. Every bone and muscle protested, but I clenched my teeth against the pain and drew my sword.

I reached out and gripped the crystal rope that now linked us together. With all my strength, I pulled her forward.

She opened her mouth to scream again, but before the sound could leave her throat, I plunged my sword deep into her rotting heart.

The hunter's red eyes flashed with anger and hatred, but it was too late for her. She sputtered and coughed, her rancid breath a whisper against my skin as she withered to nothing, her bones splintering and cracking. When her eyes went dark, I leaned against the tree and put my foot to her stomach, pulling my blade from her chest and pushing her to the ground.

As she fell, something at her neck glittered in the light. I realized whatever had originally caught my eye in the trees was now reflecting the light that shone from my diamond key.

A necklace?

Her body shook as what remained of her flesh dissolved into a thick, greenish-black liquid that bubbled like acid between her bones.

I got on my hands and knees beside her and used a stick to search through the mess of decaying matter until I found it.

A glimmering pendant made of pure white diamonds.

My pulse quickened.

Some of the more powerful hunters I'd fought in my lifetime had worn jeweled talismans. Gifts from their ruling priestess. I'd defeated hunters wearing each of the five main colors of the demon gates, but I'd never seen diamonds.

Diamonds were rumored to be the gemstone of the mysterious High Priestess. Had she been the one who sent her hunters to destroy the Southern Kingdom?

What did it mean?

I pressed a hand to my chest, wincing at the tender flesh. The diamond had somehow absorbed her attack, but it had burned the hell out of me in the process.

I didn't have time to figure it out now, but there was one thing that tugged at the edge of my thoughts.

Where the hell did Aerden get this key?

Careful not to touch it with my bare hands, I ripped a strip of cloth from the hunter's robes and wrapped it around her diamond pendant. I stuffed it in the pocket of my jeans and went to join the fight inside the domed city.

Sarra Cannon

Everything You Had

Harper

The tip of the sharp blade pierced the skin at the base of my finger, but before the hunter could push it any deeper into my flesh, her body jerked and her hand opened, her long skeletal fingers spreading wide as her blade dropped to the ground near my feet.

She grabbed at her chest, and at first, I couldn't make sense of what had happened. The world seemed to be spinning, and everything was blurry. My body was weak, and it was becoming hard to take each breath.

Something black bubbled from her chest. The hunter let out half a scream and then fell to the stones at the top of the steps, part of her robes covering my feet and legs.

I looked up and blinked through the haze. A woman with dark hair knelt at my side and placed her cool hands on my face.

"Oh, my sweet girl," she said, tears in her voice. "Hang in there. Everything's going to be okay."

Angela? I opened my mouth to try to say my sister's name, but I could no longer speak.

"Help me lay her down," she said.

A young girl with white-blonde hair came around to my other side, and I tried to smile at her. Zara.

They lifted my body and laid me down on the top of the steps near where the hunter had fallen. Angela ripped open the neck of my shirt and placed both her palms over my heart. She closed her eyes and leaned down so close I could smell the strawberry scent of her shampoo.

1 gasped for breath as the poison began to leave my system. When I opened my eyes again, my vision had cleared slightly, and I regained some of my ability to move. I lifted my hand to Zara's and squeezed her wrist, letting my head fall against her arm.

"Thank you," I whispered.

Zara and my sister had arrived just in time. They had saved my life.

But the battle wasn't over.

When I could manage it, I sat up and stared at the group of guards still fighting two hunters. Most of the shades had been destroyed, but much of my army was either dead or injured.

"Jackson," I said, trying to stand.

Zara and Angela rushed to hold me up.

"He's fine," Angela said. "We have to get you inside to safety. You're in no condition to keep fighting."

"No, I need to find him. They should be down here fighting," I said. "Where are they?"

But then, as my vision cleared a little more, I caught sight of him. He pushed his way through the guards and fell to his knees at my feet, wrapping his arms around my legs and placing his face against my stomach. His shoulders shook, and when he looked up at me, tears glistened in his eyes.

"Thank God you're okay," he said as he stood. "I was in the trees and saw the hunter. I thought I'd lost you."

I threw my arms around him and kissed the side of his neck. "I'm okay," I whispered. "We have to finish this."

"There are only two left here in the city, but Lea's also fighting one out there in the woods," he said, pulling away and looking around.

"All by herself?" I asked.

His eyes met mine and he nodded. I understood from his gaze that he had left her there.

"I'm fine, Jackson," I said. "Find Aerden. Get back out there and help her."

"There she is," Zara said, pointing to the crack in the dome.

Lea stood on the edge of the hole at the top of the shield, her bow raised. She drew back the string and sent a glimmering arrow straight into the heart of one of the two remaining hunters. They had been fighting in a group of guards and citizens, but her aim was remarkable. The hunter screeched and grasped at the arrow, greenish-black blood pulsing down the front of her robes as she fell to the street.

Lea's eyes scanned the street, but she must not have had a good angle on the last hunter, because she shifted and flew down to join the guards on the street level. She disappeared into the crowd.

There was only one hunter left, and she had managed to fight her way through the guards to the castle steps. She was only a few feet away from us when her last remaining ally fell.

She raised her arms, palms up, and took in a deep breath. Guards tried to attack her, but she had conjured a temporary shield around herself. Jackson, Zara, and I all ran toward her, our weapons ready. Jackson began casting, his hands encased in ice. He conjured a sharp spear of pure blue light, but when he threw it toward her, it merely shattered and fell to the ground like shards of glass.

None of our attacks could penetrate her shield. She had given everything she had to casting it, and my heart beat faster, wondering what she was summoning her power to do. If she set off some kind of high-level spell here, in the center of the city, with nearly all that remained of my royal guard surrounding her, she could kill them all.

"Back away," I shouted, furiously waving my hands for the guards to move back. If we couldn't get through her shield, we needed to run. "Get to safety."

A few of the guards tried one last attack, but when it failed, they obeyed me, following Gregory and the rest of the guards to safety behind a stone building farther down the street.

101

The hunter circled her hands around and around, drawing power from the world surrounding her. A furious wind began to blow, throwing debris all around us.

Jackson took my arm. "Come on," he said. "You need to stay safe, too."

I shook my head, but I knew he was right. Tears stung my eyes. This night had been disastrous. The front half of the castle was destroyed. Many of my guards were dead or injured. I had almost died, and even though Angela's healing was powerful, I still felt weak.

"I don't think I have the power to shift," I told him.

I leaned against him, allowing him to hold me up as we ran back toward the castle. Angela followed, but Zara didn't move. She seemed mesmerized.

"Zara, let's go," I shouted, turning back.

Through the rush of guards running away, I saw Lea standing in the street, attempting to raise her bow, but wincing and dropping it back down. I noticed a strip of her shirt had been torn away and wrapped around her arm, blood flowing freely from the wound despite her attempt to stop it.

Panic surged through me. Were we all going to die? Just like this? It could not end like this. I wouldn't allow it.

"Angela, Lea's hurt," I said, grabbing my sister's hand.

She turned toward Lea and nodded, shifting to white smoke and soaring toward her. She reappeared at Lea's side and Lea flinched as my sister put her hands on the wound.

I attempted to run back to pull Zara away if I had to, but I stumbled and fell. Jackson rushed to lift me up, but as I stood, I saw the hunter pause. Her head snapped toward Zara and something flashed in her eyes. She stopped casting and stood there for a moment, breathing in and out, a slow smile spreading across her decaying features.

The hunter walked forward, her shimmering shield catching the light of a nearby torch as she moved. She lifted a hand toward Zara and ran the bony remains of her fingers down her white-blonde hair. When she moved away, a thick black streak had formed in Zara's hair.

Then, without a word, she bent her knees and propelled herself upward, flying through the cracked dome and disappearing into the darkness.

Lea raised her bow, but it was too late.

I ran to Zara, taking her arm and turning her toward me. "What happened?" I said, not understanding what had just passed between them.

She had tears in her eyes and she wiped them away with the back of her sleeve. "I don't know," she said. "I was going to run up to her and see if my dagger would pierce through her shield, but when I got closer…"

Her voice cracked and she stepped toward me, pressing her face against my chest. I wrapped my arms around her and let her cry for a moment. I stroked her hair and looked around at the city, wanting to shed tears of my own.

We had survived, and the children and most of the citizens were safe inside the castle, but the dome was ruined and the blood of at least fifty soldiers ran through the cobblestone streets.

Jackson's vision had come true sooner than any of us could have imagined.

Lea and Angela walked slowly back toward us, Lea's lips pressed together in anger.

"I should have had her," she said as she reached us. "I could have pierced through her shield, I think, but I didn't have the strength. I'm so sorry."

I reached for her hand, and to my surprise, she took it. I looked into her eyes so I knew she could see that I was genuine.

"If it wasn't for you, we'd probably all be dead," I said. "Jackson told me you found another hunter in the woods. Is she dead?"

Lea nodded and pulled her hand away, turning her head to the side for a moment and taking a deep breath. "She's dead. I think she was the one attacking the dome and casting the most powerful shields, which is why no one could get through to those hunters."

I hugged Zara close and gradually, her tears subsided. She pulled away and wiped her face.

"Do you want to talk about it?" I asked. "If there's anything you saw that can help us figure out who organized this attack, maybe it will help us defend ourselves."

She sniffed and nodded. "That last hunter? When I got close to her, I recognized her," she said. "I haven't seen her for several years, but Harper, that thing used to be my Aunt Mindy. My mother's sister. Or at least I thought it was her sister. Now I know she was more like her great-great-granddaughter or something, but either way, I knew Mindy as my favorite aunt. Another third before me. She had been the one to train me as a little girl, and all the magic I learned growing up was because of her. We'd been very close, but I didn't want to contact her after my mother died. I had no idea what had happened to her."

She dissolved into tears again, and I couldn't imagine what she was going through. This poor girl had been through so much already, and to see a beloved aunt turned into such a horrible thing must have been shocking and heartbreaking.

"I'm so sorry, Zara."

"I should have at least tried to kill her with my dagger," she said. "It had belonged to my mother. What if it could have pierced through her shield?"

I shook my head and looked around at the group gathering around us. All my demon friends. The guards and the citizens who had stayed outside the castle to fight.

I realized they were all looking to me to say something, or to tell them what to do or how to begin picking up the pieces of our city.

"This is not a time to doubt or second-guess our actions," I said, struggling to speak loud enough for all to hear. "Everyone here fought with bravery and courage. You gave everything you had to save our city and our people, and while we will honor those who fell today, we will be thankful that we are still here. Still alive."

I reached for Jackson's hand and he moved to my side to steady me. I wasn't sure how much longer I'd even be able to stand.

"Willow, do you think you can patch up the primary shield of the dome for the night? At least enough to block a smaller attack, just in case the hunter who left comes back with reinforcements?"

The young girl stepped forward and nodded. "I'll do what I can," she said. "But I'm weak. It may be some time before I'm able to cast again."

"Angela," I said, turning to my sister. "Take a few of the guards and have them clear the entrance to the castle. Go down and get Courtney. She should be able to recharge Willow's power enough for her to rebuild the dome."

Angela nodded and Gregory motioned for two guards to begin clearing the main entrance to the castle.

"Anyone else who has important information about what happened can meet with Gregory tonight, if you have the strength," I said. "If you saw any clue as to which priestess these hunters were working for, like an emerald pendant or bracelet—any gemstone at all—let him know. Gregory, are you up for taking some notes tonight?"

He straightened his shoulders and bowed his head. "Of course, Your Highness."

"Thank you," I said.

"I can help," Jackson said into my ear. "I'll help get you settled inside so you can rest, and then I'll join him out here."

I nodded, wanting to seem stronger, but knowing I was still incredibly weak from the hunter's poison.

Gregory must have seen the exhaustion in my eyes. He stepped forward and leaned in so no one else could hear. "Get some rest, Princess. I'll take over from here."

I started to protest, but a wave of dizziness made me unsteady on my feet and Jackson tightened his hold on me.

"Okay," I said. "I'll be in my father's chambers. Promise you'll come get me if anything happens."

He bowed and turned to direct the people to begin cleaning up the debris and stone in the streets.

Jackson led me up the castle steps, Zara coming around to my other side to help steady me. The front entrance had been cleared, and the two of them walked with me through the throne room and up to the second floor.

I had my own suite of rooms here in the castle, but for some reason, I just wanted to feel close to my father right now. Maybe a part of me hoped that while I slept, he would come to me in my dreams, just as the cloaked woman had, and tell me what to do.

Zara kissed me on the cheek and then left us alone in my father's old bedroom. Jackson lifted me up and carefully lay me down in the soft bed. He covered me with a feathered blanket and stroked my hair, the warmth of his body comforting me as he lay at my side.

"We almost lost the city," I said, the tears I'd been holding back for hours finally falling down my cheeks and sliding back into my hair and on the pillow. "I thought everyone would be safe here, and that nothing would be able to break through those layers of shields so easily. Jackson, I—"

"Shhhh," he whispered, his mouth so close to my ear, I could feel the warmth of his breath against my neck. "Rest, my love. Just rest, and everything is going to be okay. We'll figure this out. We're survivors, remember?"

He ran a fingertip down my cheek, wiping away some of the tears. I reached out and brought his hand to my lips, and then held it close to my chest.

"There's more coming, isn't there?" I asked, my voice almost nothing in this huge, opulent room. I felt so incredibly small.

"Yes, Harper, there is more coming," he said. He placed his palm against my face and waited until I lifted my eyes to his. "But we will face it all together. And we will win."

I smiled and swiped at my eyes. What would I do without this beautiful demon in my life? I never knew I could love someone so completely.

"Get your rest," he said. "I'll come check on you when I'm done helping Gregory."

I nodded, my eyes so heavy now, I could hardly keep them open. He stood and then leaned over to kiss my forehead.

By the time he had left the room, I was already asleep.

The Key

Lea

After several hours of cleaning and dealing with the aftermath of the attack, the rest of the group took a break and sat down to dinner, but I had no appetite.

I still felt so unsettled after my close run-in with that hunter. God, she had almost killed me.

I pressed a hand to the key I still wore around my neck. I'd placed it back inside my shirt where no one else could see it, but the burns on my chest reminded me that it was there.

If it hadn't been for this key, I would be dead.

When Aerden had first given me the key, I had taken it as a token of his loyalty and friendship. At the time, I was about to become engaged to his twin brother, so it seemed appropriate and incredibly sweet.

He hadn't told me where he got it or why he chose that particular gift, only that I should keep it with me at all times and that it would keep me safe.

I had placed the key on this rope and worn it ever since, keeping it close to my heart.

Until today, it had never done anything but remind me of him. I was desperate to ask him where he had found it, but I could tell that the battle had affected him. Maybe I should have stayed with him instead of disappearing into the trees, but all I'd been able to think about was getting to a better vantage point and taking down as many of those suckers as possible.

I took a deep breath and walked through the halls of the castle. All of the children had been safely returned to their homes, and since the shield had been partially repaired, the village had grown quiet, most of the city's residents asleep in their beds.

Harper had been lucky there wasn't more damage to the castle itself. This castle had probably stood for more than a thousand years, and it would have been a shame to lose it so soon after her father's death.

I had thought taking a walk would make me feel better, but being here only reminded me of the castle I had left behind when I followed Jackson to the human world.

I was a princess, too, after all. And though I'd thought many times about going back to see my father, I had serious doubts that he would welcome me with open arms the way Harper's father had when she first arrived.

Going home was on my mind now, though. When Andros had told me about the rumors of a diamond stone guardian in the King's City of the north, I hadn't believed him. After seeing the diamond pendant on that hunter, though, I had a sick feeling in my stomach.

Was it just some kind of horrible coincidence? Or did my father have something to do with this?

I shook my head and pushed the thought aside.

The hunters belonged to the Order of Shadows, and it was believed that diamonds were the gemstone of the High Priestess. What could my father possibly have to do with her? He may be harsh and he may often make decisions that others in his kingdom don't agree with, but I knew in the deepest part of myself that he would never make an alliance with the Order of Shadows.

Still, something was eating at me.

Why bring a diamond stone guardian to his city just after he sealed the gates?

I wandered through the hallways on the main level of the castle, wishing I could make sense of what was going on.

Paintings of past kings and queens adorned the walls. Depictions of everything from great battles to serene farmland had been hung up and down every corridor. One particular painting caught my eye, and I walked over to it, pushing my own regrets deeper into my belly.

A king holding his young daughter, her smiling face tilted to his as he wrapped his arms around her.

I hadn't seen my own father in nearly thirty years.

The last time was the day I begged him to help me fight against the Order of Shadows. I had gone to him against Andros's advice. Andros had warned me that my father would never help, but I hadn't wanted to believe him. By that time, it had been almost seventy years since Aerden had been taken by the Order. Everyone believed he had become a slave in the human world and was most likely dead. And even if he wasn't dead, they all said that once taken, a demon would never be free again, but I had not been able to abandon all hope. Like Jackson, I wanted to believe we could still do something to save him.

And I wanted to save my relationship with Jackson, too.

He had followed his brother to the human world fifty years after his disappearance, fighting his way through to the other side, only to become imprisoned himself, trapped in his human form and unable to use his magic. At the time, I wasn't sure what had become of Jackson, but I could not abandon him.

Every single demon in the Shadow World had given them both up for dead, but I refused to let them go. I couldn't. I loved them both, and I couldn't imagine a life without them.

So, after decades of self-imposed exile in the Underground, far away from the safety of my father's city, I finally returned. I called a meeting with my parents and asked that Jackson and Aerden's parents be there as well. I humbled myself, begging them to help me rescue the twins we all loved so dearly.

I honestly believed they would help. Even if my father and mother were reluctant, I truly believed Jackson's parents would convince them to bring their army against the Order. How could they turn their backs on both of their sons? How could they abandon them to such torture?

And yet, that's exactly what they did.

I still didn't understand it, even after all these years.

In that moment, standing before my father's throne, my eyes had been opened to the harsh reality of love.

Love is nothing more than a word, and our actions are the only way to truly know it exists.

Staring at the painting in the great hall of Harper's castle, I wondered if I had ever been truly loved by anyone.

I wondered if Harper realized just how lucky she was to be loved by them all.

She may have grown up alone, but both of her parents had given their lives for hers. Even my beloved Jackson would gladly lay down his life for her now.

I felt so incredibly alone, and for the first time in a long time, I wondered if Andros was right. What if my place was there, with him? Fighting with the Resistance?

"I thought I might find you out here."

I turned at the sound of a familiar voice echoing off the stone walls of the great hall. I smiled at Aerden and walked over to him, pushing his long, dark hair out of his face and running a finger across the long cut at his jawline.

"Look at us," I said with a laugh, gesturing toward the bandage around my arm and the cuts on his face. "We're a mess."

"We're alive," he said. He lifted his hand and traced the spot where my fingers had touched his skin.

I looked away, unsure of the best way to approach the subject of the key. I knew he didn't like to talk about what had happened to him in the days before he'd been taken, but I needed to know.

"I wish we understood more about who had sent the hunters to attack, and why they were here," I said. "I get the feeling this was about more than just revenge."

He nodded and turned to stare at the painting on the wall beside us.

"Aerden, can I ask you something?"

"Yes," he said, turning back to me.

I hesitated, absently touching the black cord at my neck.

"Do you remember the key you gave to me just before you disappeared?" I asked softly. I held my breath, hoping he wouldn't retreat inward the way he usually did when one of us mentioned those days.

He inhaled sharply and his lips twitched. He ran a hand through his long hair and shook his head. "I haven't thought about that in a long time," he said. "Why are you asking about it now?"

I pulled the key from beneath my shirt and held it in my hand for him to see. "I've worn this every day since," I said. "But I never needed it until today."

His eyes widened and his eyes lifted to mine.

"What do you mean?"

"During the battle, I found a hunter in the trees beyond the dome," I said. "She was extremely powerful, and I'm convinced she was the one who brought down the dome itself. I also think she was the one casting those powerful shields around the other hunters."

His eyes narrowed and he reached out to touch the key. "What does that have to do with this key?" he asked.

I took a deep breath. I knew I needed to tell him, but I didn't want this information to go beyond the two of us. Until I was sure exactly what was going on, I didn't want Harper and Jackson to know that I had any suspicions about my father's possible involvement.

"Lea, what happened out there?"

"This hunter, she attacked me, and Aerden, I swear to you, if it hadn't been for this key, I wouldn't be standing here right now."

His lips parted and he took a breath. He searched my face, something I didn't understand flashing in his eyes.

"I didn't know what happened at first. One second she was sending a death blow directly at my chest, and the next, I felt this key burning into my skin," I said. "When I pulled it from under my shirt, the diamond in the center was glowing. I don't even know how to describe what happened."

111

I looked around, making sure there was no one in the hall who could hear us. I lowered my voice.

"The trail of her magic solidified," I said. "It was like the invisible residue of her spell crystallized in midair. I didn't understand it, but I took advantage of it. I grabbed the crystal rope and pulled her into my sword."

"Oh my God, Lea, I don't even know what to say," he said. "Did you tell the others about this?"

I shook my head and swallowed. "Aerden, you have to promise me you won't say anything to anyone else," I said. "I need you to do this one thing for me."

His eyebrows cinched together and he studied my face. "Why?"

"Because after the hunter died, I went back to search her body," I said. I reached into my pocket and, glancing around again to be sure we were alone, pulled out the carefully wrapped diamond pendant. "I found this."

Aerden reached for it, but I pulled it back and shook my head.

"Don't touch it," I said. "We have no idea what kind of magic might be locked inside."

His hand hovered near the pendant, and then fell to his side. "I don't understand."

"Aerden, you were there the other night when Andros told us about the stone guardian. Do you really think it's just a coincidence that two days later the Southern Kingdom gets attacked by hunters who were obviously sent here by someone who uses diamonds in their magic?"

He shook his hand and turned away. "Lea, you can't be saying you think your father had anything to do with this."

"Shh," I said, stepping toward him and placing my hand on his arm. I rewrapped the pendant and put it back in my pocket. "Please, you can't tell anyone about this."

"He would never do that," Aerden said.

"How can we possibly know what my father would or wouldn't do?" I asked. "We've been gone, Aerden. I haven't even seen him for more than thirty years, and you heard what Andros said. Everyone thinks he's gone mad, locking up the entire King's City and basically invoking martial law with the help of this dangerous stone guardian. It's crazy. We have no idea what he might be capable of."

"Lea, diamonds are known to be the gemstone of the High Priestess. Surely you don't think your father has some kind of agreement with her?"

"I don't know," I said. "But if he is somehow using diamonds to keep the demons in the city in line, I think it's entirely possible there's some connection there. Think about it. He rounded up all of the richest, most powerful demons in the Northern Kingdom and locked them inside his city where they would be safe. Everyone else? He completely abandoned them. He practically offered them up to the Order like a sacrifice to a god."

Aerden closed his eyes and turned away.

I waited as he gathered his thoughts, not sure what else there was to say or how I expected him to react to this. I guess a part of me wanted him to tell me I was crazy. That there was no way my father could be involved. But I knew that no matter what we believed, we wouldn't be sure until we'd gone looking for the truth.

"Aerden," I said. I came up behind him and touched his arm again. His muscles tensed under my touch. "I need to know where you got this key."

Sarra Cannon

The Same Fear

Harper

When I woke up, I was confused for a second about where I was. I reached to turn on the lamp, but it wasn't there.

Then, the realization of where I was, and why I was there, hit me like a freight train.

I sat up in bed, wondering how long I had slept.

I could already feel my strength returning, but the heaviness of my eyelids and the ache of my muscles told me it wasn't nearly enough. Still, there was so much work to be done on the castle, and I was dying to know if Jackson and Gregory had found out any new information about why the hunters had attacked and who had sent them here.

Although, I had a good feeling I already knew who had sent them.

I hadn't dreamt during my sleep here in my father's room, but the memory of those emeralds in the abandoned house was never far from my thoughts.

But why? Was the emerald priestess just showing us her power? Was this her way of telling us that she wanted revenge for what we had done to her sister?

Or was there more to it?

I got out of bed and walked to the other side of the room. I conjured a small orb of light and placed it inside a lamp sitting on the dresser. Above it, my father's sword hung on the wall.

When he died, he had poured most of his life force into my body, saving me from death. In the tradition of Shadow Demons, he placed what was left of his power and spirit into a stone embedded in the hilt of this sword.

I stared up at it, thinking how I needed him now more than ever.

"What should I do?" I whispered to the sword. "How do I keep them all safe?"

The door to the bedroom creaked open, and Jackson peered inside and smiled.

"You're awake," he said. "I thought you'd still be sleeping."

"How long was I out?"

"Only a few hours," he said. "How are you feeling?"

"Better. What happened with Gregory? Did you find any clues as to why the hunters were here?"

He shook his head. "No one seemed to see anything unusual other than the attack itself," he said. "We searched the bodies of the dead hunters, but didn't find any trace of a gemstone or talisman given to them by their ruling priestess."

"That's unusual, isn't it? Don't the priestesses usually give their hunters something to help increase their power?"

"Yes. And the talismans are also how the priestess tracks her hunters and controls them," he said. "It's very strange not to find a single gemstone on so many hunters."

"What about the one Lea killed in the woods?" I asked. "Did you find her body?"

"Gregory found it, but there was nothing there, either."

I closed my eyes, my head starting to pound. "We need to find the hunter who got away," I said. "She seemed to be one of the more powerful ones. What if she was the only one carrying a talisman? Unless this was some kind of band of rogue hunters, which I seriously doubt, one of them had to be carrying evidence of their master. How else would the priestess have tracked their actions?"

"I don't know," he said. "But sending someone after her could be extremely dangerous."

"Right now, it's our only chance at understanding what truly happened here tonight."

Jackson moved behind me and wrapped his arms around my waist. He leaned down and kissed my neck.

"You were looking at your father's sword?" he asked.

I nodded. "I wish he was here," I said. "He would know what to do. He might have been able to save the dome, if he had been here."

"You did a wonderful job leading the guards in battle," he said. "But I know how much you miss him. Harper, why aren't you carrying the sword? He wanted you to have it."

I looked up at the large, shining sword, and felt the tears threaten to start up again. "I don't feel like I'm ready for it, yet. Like I'm worthy of it," I said. "My father was such a great king. He knew how to protect his people and what to do in battle. He was such an incredibly strong warrior. I don't know how I could ever live up to that, Jackson. How am I—an eighteen-year-old girl with human blood running through my veins—ever going to be as great as he once was?"

Jackson turned me around to face him. "You have demon blood running through those veins, too. Royal blood," he said. "You killed one of the strongest, most powerful witches who ever lived. How can you say you aren't worthy of that sword? Do you really think you aren't good enough to be the queen of this kingdom?"

I swallowed and looked down at the floor. "Today, when the battle started and everyone was looking to me to tell them what to do, I felt like such a child," I said. "I suddenly felt like I was this tiny little person in a world bigger than anything I know how to handle. I'm not ready to be the leader they all expect me to be, Jackson. I don't know how to do this."

"Yes, you do," he said, lifting my chin with his finger. "The only thing keeping you from being what you want to be is your own inability to see what you already have become."

He leaned down and placed his lips against mine.

I put my arms around his neck and held him close, wanting nothing more than to believe him, but so incredibly terrified that he was wrong.

I went to kiss him again, but something grew warm inside the pocket of my jeans. My stomach flipped and I inhaled sharply.

I pulled away from Jackson, my jaw tense and my body trembling.

I reached inside my pocket and closed my hand around the six ruby communication stones I kept there at all times.

Please, God, not now. Don't let this be happening.

I took a deep breath, scared to open my palm for fear of what I might see.

Jackson reached to put his hand around my wrist, our eyes meeting for a brief instant, the same fear making both our hearts race.

Slowly, I opened the palm of my hand and stared down in horror at the rubies. All six of them were glowing with a bright, pulsing light. A distress call from each of the six Primas of the emerald gates who had made a secret alliance with us.

All at once, the stones went dark and shattered in my hand.

All Of Them

Lea

Two shadows flew toward us, and I quickly dropped the diamond key back inside my shirt.

Jackson and Harper took form beside us, their eyes wild and panicked.

"What's happened?" I asked, feeling my entire body tense. Had there been another attack?

"The communication stones went off," Jackson said.

"From the emerald gates?" I asked. "Which one?"

"All of them," Harper said. She held out her palm so we could see the six stones, all shattered into pieces. "Something terrible's happened. I have to get to Cypress as fast as possible."

"Lea, can you and Aerden tell the others? Send Erick, Mordecai, Joost, and Cristo out west. Ask them to check in on the gates out there," he said. "Harper and I will go to Cypress. The two of you can go to that little town outside of Atlanta and check on them."

"No, I want Lea with me," Harper said. "If something has happened to Eloise and her girls, I want to have Lea pull up the memories of what happened."

I nodded. "I'll go with Harper," I said. "Jackson, you can go with Aerden and rally the others. We'll spread out and see what we can find at each of the gates."

"What do we do about the castle?" Jackson asked. "We can't leave it undefended."

"Tell Angela to stay here with the guards," Harper said. She pulled several small leather bags out of a large backpack she must have grabbed from her rooms here in the castle. She removed one ruby from each small bag and handed them to Jackson. "Pass these stones out to everyone. Make sure Angela has one so she can contact us if something happens here in the castle. And make sure to keep one for yourself."

"I think we should tell everyone to be very careful at each of these gates," I said. I knew I was keeping things from them about this most recent attack, and the last thing I wanted was for us to split up and come across a more dangerous foe than anyone was prepared for. "We don't know what's happened or why, but the fact that it comes on the heels of this attack on the castle makes me suspicious. Sneak in wherever you go and don't alert anyone to your presence until you know the coast is clear."

Harper nodded. "That's a good idea," she said. She gripped Jackson's arm and leaned over to kiss him. "Contact me as soon as you know something in Atlanta."

I looked away, and found that Aerden was staring at me.

"We'll talk about it later?" he asked softly.

I gave a simple nod, and followed Harper out to the portal inside the white roses that would take us back to Brighton Lake.

Aerden hadn't had a chance to answer about the diamond key, and now that we were splitting up, I had no idea when I would have the opportunity to ask him about it again. If we found any evidence that the High Priestess had anything to do with these six communication stones going dark, I knew I would have no choice but to tell Harper the truth.

For now, though, I wanted to hold onto this information awhile longer.

If my father was truly involved in some way, I had to be sure before I gave it over to Harper to deal with.

I didn't like the idea of her making decisions about how to handle my own father. This was my problem to deal with for now, and I'd tell her only if it became completely necessary.

As soon as I could, I would find Aerden alone and ask him again about the key. If whatever he had to say led me back to my father's castle, then I would start making preparations to leave and join Andros and the Resistance once again.

Sarra Cannon

Until It Was Too Late

Harper

I grabbed a few supplies from my room and started up the stairs to the third floor.

"Where are you going?" Lea asked.

"I'm using the Hall of Doorways."

She shook her head. "No, I don't think that's a good idea," she said. "There's a reason we haven't been using those doors, Harper."

"I know, but if Cypress and the other gates are under attack, we don't have any time to lose. It's a four-hour drive to Cypress," I said, hating that I was wasting my time arguing with her instead of already through to Eloise's house. "If something has happened to them, the Order probably already knows we're heading that way, anyway. Using the doors isn't going to change that."

"Right now, we don't know anything," she said. "Trust me when I say that the element of surprise can often be one of the only advantages you have in battle. Never give that up unless you have to."

"What other choice do we have? We can't sit in a car for four hours and hope they're okay," I said, my cheeks flushed. "They could die while we're on the highway. These people are my family."

"I get that," she said. "But you have to think of the big picture, here. If you use those doors, the Order will most likely know instantly that we're there. If they have an entire army sitting there in Cypress, we're both dead. Or worse. Is that what you want?"

I closed my eyes and pressed my hand against the wall. My head was throbbing. I was starting to regret asking her to come with me.

"No, but I don't want my friends to die, either."

"They may already be dead," she said.

My jaw tensed and I stared her down. How could she be so cold? Sometimes she could seem so heartless.

"They're not dead," I said. "I would know if they were. I can still feel their demon. He's a part of me, remember?"

She nodded. "Okay, so hold onto that," she said. "Use that as your guide right now. If he's still alive, that means Eloise is still alive, too."

I listened, and maybe part of me knew she was right. I was the one who had made the rule about not using the Hall of Doorways for our travels, but this was an emergency. How else would we get there?

"We'll fly," I said, pushing past her and running down the stairs. "They can track us later, but they won't be able to sense us coming."

She nodded. "Okay. Let's go."

I opened the front door of Brighton Manor and shifted to smoke, flying high into the air like a bird. I found the current above the clouds and pushed my demon form as hard as I ever had, crossing miles in seconds.

When we reached Cypress, I was exhausted, but determined to find Eloise. Lea and I reformed a few blocks away from the Prima's house in a dark alleyway downtown.

The darkness was absolute, coating us in shadow. I pulled my black hoodie over my head and peered around the corner toward the deserted street.

I counted to ten, my eyes searching for any sign of movement. The rattle of a plastic bag caught on a tree limb. A black cat slinking into the alley down the street. The flutter of bird wings above my head.

But it was completely silent and still. There was no movement at all on the street. Not a single car or person or animal in sight.

Lea touched my arm, and I jumped, gasping and then clutching my chest.

"You scared the crap out of me," I said.

"It's so quiet," she said. "Something's not right here. Did you notice when we were flying that there were no birds up there? Nothing."

I shook my head. "I guess I was only thinking about getting here," I said. "Eloise's house is just a few blocks away. Let's go there first."

With no sign of human face or footstep, I shifted and darted across the street, my heart racing until we'd reached the safety of the next shadowed place.

Lea was right. There was no movement or noise along the next street either. I hadn't stopped to check what time it was, but even though it was late, something about the stillness of this town weighed on me. Not one car drove along the streets of this place. Lights were on in a few houses, but no shadows moved past the windows. There was no movement anywhere.

Something definitely wasn't right.

Fear welled inside me like a stone, growing heavier with each step we took toward the Prima's house.

I rested my palms against the rough bark of the oak tree behind her home, watching. A single light burned on the front porch, but the windows were dark. What was going on in this town?

I glanced toward Lea, who was standing beside a tree a few steps back. I jerked my head toward the house and she nodded. We both shifted and reformed in the shadows near the back porch.

I wrapped the edge of my black cloak around my hand and tried to turn the knob, but it was locked. I closed my eyes and took a deep breath, trying to calm myself enough to feel the life of the earth beneath me. Sometimes it was a challenge to be half-human, half-demon, because the powers worked differently in each world. Learning to switch between them had taken practice, and when I was upset or worried, it took longer for me to connect to the core of my magic.

After what felt like an eternity, I finally felt the tingle of energy rush along my skin. I focused on the lock inside the house, using my mind to turn it upward. When I heard it click, I opened the back door and slipped inside.

It opened easily, the murmur of a groan coming from the hinges.

"Eloise?" I whispered.

The darkness answered back with a silence so complete, it deafened me. Usually houses had a sound. The buzz of a refrigerator or the whirring of the air conditioning. There was nothing here but silence. Goose bumps broke out along my arms.

Careful of each footfall, I continued deeper into the house. My shoulders ached with tension. Every muscle in my body was on alert, ready to flee or fight.

I had just been in this house hours ago, but it felt like weeks after what we'd been through. Had my visit here somehow put her in more danger? Had someone followed me?

And why would all six of the stones have gone off at once? No one but the group living in Brighton Manor knew the identities of those who had agreed to join our cause. How would the Order have known to coordinate an attack on just those six gates? Unless someone in our group had betrayed us.

My body went cold.

Betrayal was something I'd grown all too familiar with in my lifetime. It was my fatal flaw, and I never saw it coming until it was too late. People I considered great friends and allies had turned their backs on me when I needed them most. But the thought of someone inside the Demon Liberation Movement giving us up to the Order? The thought chilled me to the bone.

I pushed it all away, focusing only on finding my friends and figuring out what the hell happened. Part of me prayed the stones had somehow malfunctioned. Maybe they had been damaged in the attack, and I would find Eloise and her daughters sleeping safely upstairs.

As I passed through the kitchen, I could picture her there with me last night, handing me the gift of her wedding veil.

Please, let them be okay.

I moved faster, my footsteps a whisper on the carpeted staircase.

I reached Eloise's bedroom at the top of the stairs first. The door was open, and the light was off. I stepped inside and called her name again.

"Eloise," I whispered. I took a deep breath and hoped that when I flipped on the light, she would simply sit up, rub her eyes, and ask what in the world I was doing here so late.

My hands trembled as I reached for the light switch.

I flicked it up, but Eloise was not in her bed. The covers were rustled, as if she'd been sleeping there moments before, but there was no other sign of her. I knew her husband was off on a business trip for a few more days, but where was she?

"She's not here," I called down to Lea. She was still downstairs, staring at something in the living room. "Caroline's room is down the hall."

I practically ran to my friend's room, not bothering to call her name before I flipped on the light. Her room looked exactly the same. She was gone, but her bed wasn't made. It was as if they'd been taken in their sleep.

I passed Meredith's room since she had gone away to college, and opened the final door—the guest room where Sophie was staying. Praying for answers, I pushed the door open.

This room was not empty.

Sitting in the center of the room was an iron cage exactly like the one I'd seen in my dream just a few nights earlier. I flipped the light on and rushed toward it. Sophie was sitting inside, her knees pulled up to her chest as she sobbed.

When she lifted her face, she had scratches all down her cheeks. Blood had dried across her arms and legs, long gashes running from nearly head to toe.

"Lea, in here," I shouted. "Sophie, are you okay? I'm going to get you out of there."

"Harper?" she asked, reaching her hand forward as if to search the air. She touched an iron bar and wrapped her hand around it, pulling herself forward. "Is that you?"

"Yes, it's me, sweetheart," I said, already fiddling with the lock. "I'm going to get this lock open. What happened? Where's Eloise?"

Sophie searched for my hand, as if she couldn't see to tell exactly where I was. When I stared into her eyes, I noticed they were unfocused and bloodshot.

I couldn't open the lock with magic. I dropped it and sat back on the floor of the room, wanting to cry. We were being attacked on every side, and I still didn't have the first clue what was going on or what their real plan was.

"Sophie, you have to tell me where Eloise is," I said.

She began to sob again, leaning her head against the bars. "They're gone," she said. "They're all gone."

"What do you mean they're gone? Who took them?"

"I couldn't see," she said through her tears. "They blinded me when they came in, and I still can't see a thing. Help me, please. It hurts to be in here. I feel like I'm suffocating."

I stared at the cage, trying to figure out how I could get this girl out of there. The only other time I'd seen cages like this outside of my dreams was in the basement of Priestess Winter's home, Winterhaven. She used them to turn human witches into hunters, and if I had to guess, I would say the suffocating feeling Sophie had was because the steel of these cages was enchanted with some kind of soul stone that slowly drained her power and life from her body.

If we didn't get her out of there soon, she would begin to turn into one of those awful things we had just faced in the Shadow World. I couldn't let that happen to her.

Then I remembered how I'd gotten my sister out of the cage when I'd found her inside.

"Sophie, do you have any bobby pins? Or a pendant with some kind of sharp piece that would fit inside this lock?"

She nodded and pointed to her dresser. I found an emerald scarab pendant in her jewelry box and used the sharp end to pick the lock. It clicked open and the girl fell out into my arms.

Lea came running into the room and knelt down beside me. "There's something else you need to see," she whispered into my ear.

"What is it?" I asked.

"Harper…" Sophie's voice drifted off and her eyes closed. She slumped over, her head falling against my chest.

I rocked her back and forth and her eyes fluttered open.

"Thank you," she said.

"Sophie, did the people who came here say anything else to you? Did they say why they were here? Or where they were taking Eloise and her daughter?"

"They said to give you this," she said, her voice so soft, I had to struggle to hear her. She held a closed fist out toward me, and then opened her palm and showed me a small emerald. "I couldn't see her, but the woman who was here told me you'd come. She said to give you a message."

I swallowed and took the jewel from Sophie's hand. "What message?"

She passed out before she could answer, but I didn't need her to tell me. The moment I touched the jewel, my vision went black and a woman's face appeared before me.

"You took someone precious from me," she said, her green eyes shining with light. "Now, I'm going to teach you what it feels like to have everyone and everything you love ripped from your life in the blink of an eye. My sister was powerful, but she was foolish. You won't find me so easy to destroy."

She faded into the darkness and my sight returned. I dropped the emerald to the floor, my hands shaking uncontrollably.

So far she had nearly destroyed my father's castle, killed half of my guards, and kidnapped the only woman I'd ever thought of as a mother. Where would it end? And how would we all possibly survive it?

Sarra Cannon

What Kind Of Power

Lea

I wanted to shake her. Harper could be so foolish sometimes.

She'd just grabbed that stone like it was nothing, not even thinking about what it might do to her. It could have killed her on contact.

She was always risking her life, thinking only of how to save her friends, and while that may have seemed heroic to everyone else, I wished she realized just how much putting her own life in danger affected our entire group. Without her, we never would have defeated Priestess Winter in the first place.

If she got hurt or died now, there was no telling if we would be able to defeat the rest of the Order.

"Are you okay?" I asked.

She nodded and rubbed a hand across her forehead. She was cradling the injured human girl, checking to make sure she was still breathing. "I'll be fine," she said. "We need to get her to Angela as soon as we can. You had something else you wanted to show me first?"

I glanced at the girl, trying to make sense of what I'd seen downstairs.

"Come with me."

I held out a hand to help Harper stand. She lay the girl on a pillow and followed me down the stairs to the living room.

"Look at the clock," I said.

She lifted her eyes to a clock on the wall above the fireplace. "What about it?"

"Notice how none of the hands are moving?"

She nodded. "Maybe it needs new batteries?"

"I don't think so," I said. "When we first came in, I noticed the one in the kitchen wasn't working, either."

"What are you getting at?" she asked, fatigue heavy in her voice.

"You don't think it's weird that we saw no birds when we were flying? That when we came into town, not a single car was on the road? And now, all the clocks in this house are stuck at exactly three a.m., the most powerful time for a witch's power in this world?"

She took a deep breath and studied the clock again. "What does it mean?"

"Don't you notice how everything is completely quiet? No sound at all? I noticed it immediately, and I don't think it's just that this clock needs new batteries."

"I don't understand what you're saying," Harper said.

"Follow me." I walked to the front door and swung it open, looking both ways down the street.

"What are you looking for?" she asked.

"Proof," I said. "Come on."

She glanced back toward the stairs. "We can't just leave her up there," she said. "She's injured."

"She's sleeping. And right now, there are more important things at stake than the life of that one girl."

I walked down the street until I saw something in the neighbor's yard that made my heart stop. "There," I said, pointing to the cat.

A black cat on the neighbor's porch was frozen with one paw on the top step. I counted to ten, but the cat never moved.

"What the hell is going on?" Harper asked, fear in her voice.

I ran up the stairs of the house and pushed open the door.

"Lea, you can't just go walking into some stranger's house in the middle of the night," Harper called from a few steps behind me.

"If I'm right, they'll never know I was here."

I searched the house, pointed out another clock stopped at three on the dot. I ran up the stairs, Harper at my heels. In one of the bedrooms, I found a couple in their bed. I flicked on the lights and they didn't move.

The woman was sleeping on her side, but the man had been just about to get out of bed. Who knows, maybe he'd needed to go to the bathroom in the middle of the night. Or maybe he'd heard a strange noise. But he was motionless now, frozen in time, his eyes wide open and one foot on the floor.

I walked in front of him and waved my hand up and down in front of his face.

"Oh my God," Harper said in a whisper, bringing her hand to her mouth. "They're frozen."

She rushed out of the room and back down the stairs. I followed her and watched as she looked up in the sky and all around.

"Look," she said, pointing upward.

Above us, a black crow was suspended, wings outstretched, unmoving.

I turned in a circle, noticing all the clues we'd missed on our way into town. No wind was blowing. The trees were completely silent and unmoving. It was an unnatural stillness that was definitely no coincidence.

"The world has completely stopped," I said. "I think whoever did this froze time."

"That's impossible," Harper said. "Something like that would take an insane amount of power."

"Not if it's just this one town," I said. "A single witch could freeze time in a radius around her for several hours if she possessed the right abilities and conserved enough of her power."

Harper pulled a communication stone from her pocket. It was glowing a bright red and she waved her hand over the top of it, activating its power.

"Harper, something horrible has happened," Jackson's voice said through the stone. "Aerden and I are here near Atlanta and I can't explain it, but everything has just stopped, as if the whole world froze in an instant. The Prima's gone."

133

Harper's face went white and she looked up at me, panic wild in her eyes.

"It's the same thing here," she said. "Get everyone to Brighton Manor as fast as you can."

Harper put the stone back in her pocket and turned in circles, dropping the black hood from her long blonde hair. When she stopped turning, she looked at me, shaking her head.

"What about freezing the entire world?" she asked. "What kind of power would it take to do that?"

I took a deep breath and stared at her, wishing I had the answers. I thought again of the High Priestess and the power she was rumored to have.

"It's impossible," I said.

"Then how is this happening?" she asked, lifting her hands and motioning to the silent street.

"I don't know," I said. "But I'm going to find out."

A Frozen Town

Lea

"Just give me a few minutes alone," I said. "Go sit with the girl. If she wakes up, see if you can find out why she's the only one who isn't affected by this spell. I'll come find you when I'm done. We'll go through it again if I find anything I can't explain on my own."

Harper walked back into the Prima's house, and I made my way into the middle of the street in front. Where to start?

If someone from the Order had physically come here to stop time, give Sophie a message, and kidnap the Prima and her family, they most likely would have come through the Hall of Doorways.

I would start there.

I followed Harper into the house. I found the secret doorway that led up to the attic. Every Prima's house had one of these secret doors. The first room was in the shape of a pentagram with five doors. One usually led to some kind of library where the Primas kept their spellbooks and journals. Another was often some kind of laboratory where they could brew potions and stock ingredients for various spells.

But the door I wanted was the one with a symbol on the front. The symbol varied depending on the special ability or spirit animal of the family. Most Prima families had a demon on their door.

I took a deep breath and closed my eyes. To cast my power in the human world, I had to steal power from something living. I was careful not to draw my power from Harper or Sophie, since I knew they were already weakened. Instead, I reached out, searching for something I could afford to kill or harm.

A large oak tree towered over the Prima's house. It would be a shame to lose something so beautiful that had stood for so many years, and it would leave a mark that couldn't be explained easily if anyone came looking, but it was my best option.

I fed my power through the earth until it connected to the tree. It was like plugging in to a living thing, siphoning its energy through a thin magical thread. When I had enough, I began conjuring the scene, my mind exploring the past hour since the communication stones had gone off.

Nothing happened.

I took another deep breath and tried again, but I hit the same wall of darkness.

One of my special abilities was the power to conjure memories. The more emotionally or magically charged the event, the easier it was to see it. Usually.

I had no doubt whatever happened in this world over the past hour or so of time was caused by an immensely powerful type of magic, so the fact that I couldn't see anything had me freaking out.

I placed my hand on the door itself, hoping maybe some physical contact with the location might help, but again my magic was denied, only darkness consuming my visions.

I raced back down the stairs and decided to try another tactic. Maybe there was something about the pentagon room that was making it difficult for me to cast.

I walked back out into the night and stood on the front lawn of the Prima's house. I crouched low and put my hands on the ground, drawing more energy from the grass and critters living inside the earth.

I reached back farther in time. Since we had been caught up in the attack most of the night, we had no idea when things had started to go wrong here in Cypress. Maybe whatever happened had begun hours earlier?

I closed my eyes and reached back for any emotion or magic that happened here in the past twenty-four hours that I might be able to latch onto.

It worked. A memory pushed into my brain and I held onto it, like wrapping my hands around that moment in time. In my vision, the street was dark. I wasn't sure what time it was, but it was late enough to be dark and early enough that most of the lights were still on in all the nearby houses. A car raced past me on the street.

A dark figure caught my eye, crossing the street a few houses down. She glanced behind her and walked quickly toward me. When she turned her head forward, I saw her and realized I had gone back to about seven or eight the previous night.

The girl in black was Harper, coming to see Eloise. I fast-forwarded the vision, something my father had taught me to do. Out of every demon I had ever known, he was the only one who could reach back in time and conjure memories the way I could.

I watched as Harper left the house an hour later and disappeared into the shadows between two houses. The memories firm in my mind, I walked toward the house. Sometimes moving around inside the visions caused them to break, but if I wanted to know what had happened here, I knew I needed to be inside where I could see the Prima.

Nothing strange happened for a while. Eloise cleaned the kitchen and went upstairs to say goodnight to the girls. Sophie disappeared into her room and a little while later, most of the lights in the house had gone dark.

I looked at one of the clocks, pushing forward until just before three.

But the moment the clock struck three in the morning, I hit a wall. Everything around me froze. I spun in circles as I tried to force my magic forward, but I must have pushed too hard, because the vision ceased to exist in my mind and all that remained was darkness.

I clenched my jaw and expanded the reach of my connection, wondering if the oak tree and grass had provided all it could, cutting my magic off mid-scene. But when I connected to a cluster of pine trees lining the backyard, the scene would not return.

Frustrated, I pushed everything I had into the scene, but it was no use. All I saw was darkness.

Stopping time shouldn't have made the memory go dark, no matter how powerful the spell. I'd conjured memories of frozen time before and had clearly been able to see the world frozen before me. Something was different this time.

My magic had been purposely blocked.

My hands fell to my side and the memory dropped from my vision. Fear knotted in my stomach as I studied the current scene. A frozen town. A Prima taken in the middle of the night. A girl left behind with a warning meant for Harper.

The witch who cast this spell had known we were coming.

More importantly, they seemed to know about my unique power to replay the past events of any place or object. Whatever they'd done after they froze time, they didn't want me to know about it.

Other than my father, a few members of the Resistance, and the friends I lived with at Brighton Manor, I thought no one knew of my ability to conjure memories.

I looked back toward the secret doorway leading to the attic and cold shivers ran down my spine. Whoever did this had ties with someone close to me.

I Want You To Be Surprised

Harper

Sophie slept in my arms. She'd been badly scratched all over her body, but why? Had she struggled when they'd tried to put her in the cage?

This poor girl had already been through so much, it hurt my heart to think what she must be feeling. We needed to get her to my sister as soon as possible so her wounds could be healed. I hoped Courtney would be able to restore whatever power had been siphoned from her inside the cage, as well.

I rocked the girl back and forth, waiting for Lea to come back.

Jackson's words kept ringing in my ears. *Everything has stopped, as if the whole world froze in an instant.*

Who could possibly be powerful enough to stop the entire world?

And how could we have hope of defeating someone like that?

Lea appeared in the doorway of Sophie's bedroom, and I looked up at her expectantly, but she shook her head.

"I couldn't see anything," she said. "Someone's blocked my magic. All I can see is darkness."

"It has to be the emerald priestess casting this magic," I said. "We need to get back to Brighton Manor and figure out what we're going to do about it and how we're going to get my friends back."

"Do you think they were the only ones taken?" she asked.

"What do you mean?" I moved from under Sophie, laying her head gently back down on a pillow I had brought over from her bed.

"I mean, there were how many other witches in this town? Hundreds, right? Cypress is slightly bigger than Peachville and there were several hundred members of the Order living there when the coven was still active," she said. "Were Eloise and her daughter the only ones kidnapped? Or was every witch in this town taken, too?"

I whimpered and stood, holding onto the side of the dresser. "I hadn't even thought of that," I said. "Eloise has a list of all her members upstairs in the library, along with their current addresses. I'll go find it. Can you stay with Sophie?"

Lea nodded and paced the room.

I found the secret door to the attic and walked up the narrow steps to the first room. Eloise had brought me here a few times before to show me some of the spells she kept in her grimoire. I opened the first door to my left and studied the shelves. There had to be at least a thousand books in this room, and I knew from my own experiences in the library at Brighton Manor that there was a system to finding the one you wanted.

A small table near the bookshelves held a golden pen, emeralds embedded in its side. I picked it up and a trail of shimmering light followed its movement through the air.

Carefully, I wrote out the word "Cypress Directory" across the air. The shimmering light spelled out the words I'd written. A book near the very top popped out of the row and floated down toward me. I opened it and turned to the most recent entries.

There were currently three hundred and twelve names listed as active members of the Cypress coven, their daughters' names written beside them, with their age and status marked in a faintly glowing green ink.

I set the pen back down on the table and scanned for Eloise's street name among the addresses. I needed to find the closest house. My finger landed on one just a few numbers down.

I memorized a few of the other addresses on this street and set the book on the floor.

"I found one," I said to Lea. "I'm going to check it. I'll be right back."

I shifted to white smoke. I soared down the stairs, out onto the porch, and down the street until I found the house marked 1216 Murray Lane. With my heart beating quicker, I entered the house. As I passed by the living room, I saw a man sitting in a recliner with his feet up. His eyes were open and the TV was on, but he didn't move at all and the image on the TV was unchanging, an ad for a local pizza delivery frozen on the screen.

I moved up the steps toward the bedrooms. In one, I found a young boy, sleeping peacefully but not moving.

I closed his door and opened the next. A girl's room for sure, decorated all in pink and purple with at least a dozen Hello Kitty dolls lining her bookshelves. Her bed was empty, and my heart sank.

I remembered seeing in the directory that Sonora Wesley, age thirty-two, had one daughter. Ashley, age six. Her status had been marked with a circle. I wasn't sure what that meant, but I'd noticed that most girls over the age of thirteen were marked with a green check, probably indicating that they were already trainees of the Order.

Other younger girls had been marked with an x, and I wondered if that meant they didn't possess any magical abilities? Or if the Order had chosen some other method of rejecting them. What must a mother feel when her daughter was marked with an x? Relief? Or disappointment?

I guessed it depended on the type of mother she was. If I'd had a daughter, I would have prayed for the Order to pass her by and let her live her own life.

Sonora's daughter had not been so lucky.

I found her mother's room and confirmed that Sonora was also missing.

Just to be sure, I quickly checked the houses of several other witches nearby. At the next house, an elderly woman had been boiling water for tea, but the bubbling liquid and the woman were frozen in place, her hand holding a tea bag by its string. Her daughter, a twenty-eight-year old witch named Bonnie, was gone.

In every house, I found the same thing. Anyone not listed in the directory or marked with an *x* was still there, but all of the witches who were either members, trainees, or marked with a circle were gone.

The Order had kidnapped all three hundred and twelve members, plus their young daughters. What could they possibly want with that many witches? If the same thing had happened in each of the six towns who had allied themselves with us, that meant over two or three thousand witches had been taken in an instant.

But where? And more importantly, why?

I shivered and pushed back the tears that sprang to my eyes. This was my fault. These witches had joined our cause and trusted me to keep them safe and to guide them. Now, they were prisoners of war.

The fact that this happened just hours after a large-scale attack on my father's kingdom in the Shadow World made me sick to my stomach.

In my dreams, someone had been trying to warn me about all of this. Somehow the emerald priestess was involved, but was she really so much more powerful than her own sister? Priestess Winter had been the oldest of the five sisters who started the Order of Shadows. I had hoped that also meant she was the strongest and most powerful.

If we put an end to her, we had hope of also destroying her sisters.

But this? An army of hunters in the Shadow World, strong enough to bring down my protective dome and nearly destroy my city. A spell powerful enough to stop possibly the entire world in its tracks.

How the hell were we going to get out of this?

I started up the stairs to Eloise's house, but a glint of green stopped me in my tracks. There, on the swing right on the front porch, was another small emerald stone. I could have sworn it wasn't here before.

142

I glanced around, wondering if someone was here with us, watching us.

I sat down and took a deep breath before picking up the stone and holding it in my hand.

Once again, my vision went black and the woman's face appeared. This time, she was smiling.

"By now, you've realized that every witch in this town is gone," she said. "Including your precious friends. For every hour I don't have what I want, one of these witches will die, a sacrifice to the spell that's holding the world suspended in time. I need something to fuel it, after all, and what better way than the death of traitors? Their deaths are on you, Harper, which I just know is going to eat you alive inside. And don't bother wondering what it is I'm after."

A thin smile stretched across her lips.

"I want you to be surprised."

Sarra Cannon

An Agenda

Harper

"They're all gone," I said to Lea when I went back up to Sophie's room. "I didn't check every house, obviously, but there's no doubt the witches listed in the directory are missing, along with all of their young daughters listed as trainees or possible future trainees."

"We have to assume that's happened in every demon gate town," Lea said. She shook her head. "I don't know how this is possible. Stopping time in a specific place for a short period of time has been done, but I never dreamed anyone was capable of stopping time in several places at once."

"We need to get back to Brighton Manor to talk this out," I said. "And we need to figure out just how much of the world is affected."

She nodded and lifted the sleeping girl from the floor. I reached to help but she motioned me away. "I'll carry her," she said. "You need to save your strength."

I moved toward the stairs, but Lea stopped me.

"We'll use the Hall of Doorways," she said. When I raised an eyebrow, she said, "They already know we're here."

We both shifted to shadow and flew up the secret stairway and into the long corridor of doors. It had been a long time since I'd set foot in the Hall of Doorways, and goose bumps rose on my flesh.

Just the thought of all the witches beyond these doors and their collective evil being used to manipulate everything in this world from fame to politics made my skin crawl.

Somewhere, behind one of the doors, was the home of the witch who had cast this spell and kidnapped my friends. Where was she keeping them? That was something else I needed to discuss with the others. Where could you possibly hide thousands of people? One home wouldn't be large enough to contain so many, even if they were sleeping or frozen in time.

After a few minutes of searching, we found the Peachville door, marked with a demon's face.

We stepped through the door and when we'd reached the second floor of my house, I felt overcome by fear.

I'd felt safe here for months. We'd all worked to restore the house and build a life here. When the sapphire gates fell, I'd had Willow and some other powerful casters come to place a protective barrier around the entire property. It protected the house, and more importantly, it protected the secret portal to the domed city in the Southern Kingdom.

No one could enter the barrier without being accompanied by someone who lived here. Not even the postman.

But after what had happened to the dome in the Southern Kingdom, I knew we weren't safe. We might at least have some warning of an attack, but I was sure it was coming.

Mary Anne, Essex, Zara, and Courtney were waiting for us in the kitchen, fresh coffee filling the air with its welcome smell. There was no sign of Jackson, Aerden, and the other four demons.

Startled, I stared at Zara. More than half of her hair was now jet black. Her usually glowing skin had become duller, and a strange dark vein had appeared on her neck, snaking up from her shirt. What was happening to her?

"I'm so glad you're home," Mary Anne said, standing to give me a hug. "What the heck is going on? Jackson told us to come here and wait for word, but we saw some pretty strange stuff in the woods when we came through the portal."

"So it's happening here, too?" I asked.

Footsteps sounded on the stairs and Jackson and Aerden appeared in the doorway to the kitchen. I walked over to Jackson and threw my arms around him.

"I can't believe this is happening," I said against his ear. "What are we going to do?"

"We're going to figure this out together," he said, pulling away and squeezing my hand.

"Everyone grab some coffee and something to eat if you're hungry. I don't think we're going to be getting much sleep for a while, and we really need to talk."

"What about Angela?" Jackson asked when everyone got up and started making plates of food. "Shouldn't she be here, too?"

"I need her there to help keep the Southern Kingdom safe for now," I said. "We'll fill her in later. I'll need her to come help Sophie. She's beat up pretty badly."

"Sophie?" he asked. "She wasn't taken?"

I shook my head. "She's here. I'll explain when everyone's listening."

Once we were all settled around the table, I started the meeting.

"A very powerful spell seems to be holding the world suspended in time. As far as we know, all the Primas and members of the six covens who joined our alliance have been kidnapped. It's hard to tell if they were taken in groups or all at the same time, but it's obvious they were taken by surprise, and without any apparent struggle."

"And they knew we were coming," Lea said. "My ability to see the events of the past connected to that place has been blocked. I never even knew that was possible."

"Do you think the emerald priestess is behind this?" Mary Anne asked.

"Yes," I said. "She left a message for me with the girl upstairs."

All eyes turned to me.

"When I got to Cypress, Eloise and Caroline were gone, but I found Sophie locked inside an iron cage, just like the one I rescued my sister from in the basement at Winterhaven a few months ago."

Zara gasped and pulled a hand to her mouth. "How would they have gotten in without me knowing?" she asked. "I conjured specific warning spells at every entrance to that house so that if anyone came inside, I'd know about it."

"I'm not sure," I said. "Maybe those kinds of warnings don't work against the emerald priestess. Maybe she dispelled them before she went in, but I'm positive that cage came from her house."

"Is she okay? The girl, I mean," Zara asked. She coughed and ran a hand over her forehead.

"She's scratched up and can't see. She's very weak, but she's alive. Courtney, after the meeting is done, can you go up and see if you can help restore her power?" I asked.

Courtney pushed her hair out of her face and nodded.

"Thank you."

"You said this girl was some kind of clue that led you to believe the emerald priestess was responsible for this?" Aerden asked. He threw a glance toward Lea that I couldn't read.

"She handed me an emerald stone with a message inside," I said. I looked over at Jackson. "The emerald priestess appeared to me and said that I had taken someone precious from her, so in return she was going to take everyone I cared about away from me."

I pressed my lips together and looked down at the table, stifling the tears that threatened to fall. Someone had already taken Eloise and Caroline. They probably had Meredith, too. I couldn't let them take the people in this room away from me, too. I wouldn't survive it.

"There was a second message on the porch when I came back from the houses of the other witches in town, just to see if they were gone," I said.

Lea's head snapped up. "What? Why didn't you tell me that? Maybe whoever left it was still in that town, Harper."

I shook my head and pushed my hair back from my face. "We weren't prepared for another fight, Lea," I said.

"What did the second message say?" Jackson asked.

"That for every hour she didn't get what she wanted, she would kill another witch from the emerald gates," I said. "To keep her spell running. She said this was all my fault."

"What does she want?" Aerden asked.

"She said she wanted me to be surprised."

"Well, that's just lovely," Mary Anne said, rolling her eyes. "We could all use a little more surprise in our lives, right? Because two attacks in one night isn't enough."

"We need to keep eyes on Brighton Manor and the Southern Kingdom," I said. "If she wants something we have, those are the two places she'll come looking."

"In her messages, did she ever say she was responsible for the attack on the domed city?" Jackson asked.

"She didn't have to," I said. "It's obvious, isn't it? The guards may not have found any emerald summoning stones, but I think we know for sure who sent those hunters to attack us."

Aerden and Lea shared another pointed look.

"What?" I asked. "If you guys know something, you need to tell us."

Lea shook her head, but I got the feeling she was holding something back. She didn't trust me to lead this group, and I could see it in her eyes.

I hated that there was this tension between Lea and me, but I had no idea how to fix it. Not without giving up Jackson, and that was something I could never do.

"There's something else that's been bothering me," I said. "How did she find out about our alliances? The emerald gates have been very careful to carry out their duties as ordered so no one would be suspicious. Other than Eloise, only the people living in this house knew which gates had joined us."

"Are you suggesting one of us told them?" Lea asked. "That's ridiculous."

"I hope so," I said. "But I've been blindsided before by people who claimed to be loyal friends and turned out to be working for my greatest enemy."

"Still, everyone here has proved themselves over and over," Lea said. "Maybe Eloise told them."

My jaw tensed and I bit down on the inside of my lip. "Eloise did not tell them," I said. "In case you forgot, she fought on our side during the last battle. Also, she'd be putting her own life in danger, since she's part of the alliance. It had to have been someone else."

"Maybe they were watching all along," Aerden said. He rarely spoke in our group meetings, and I was surprised to hear him talk.

"How?"

He closed his eyes and pressed two fingers to his forehead, as if he'd suddenly been overcome by a terrible headache. "My memories of those years have been jumbled in my head for the last few months," he said. "But after that fight tonight, some things have become clearer."

He didn't expand on what he meant by that, but I could tell he was wrestling with something.

"I remember this feeling of the Primas I lived inside always being worried that the Order was watching them," he said. It was the most he had ever said about his time as a slave to the Order. "It was a constant fear. They were never sure how their priestess was spying on them, only that there were too many instances of Priestess Winter knowing exactly what was going on in their coven for her not to be listening."

"That would have been awesome to know before we met with the Primas," Mary Anne mumbled.

I closed my eyes and let my head fall into my hands. This whole time we'd been careful not to be seen meeting with a Prima. We'd used glamours and other disguises. We often set up meetings miles away from their towns, thinking that would keep us all safe.

I'd never thought of the possibility that the Order would still be listening to everything we said. What if they'd been watching us the whole time through something the Primas wore or something similar to the tattoo the Order gave to recruits? The emerald priestess was right. This was my fault.

"What do we do now?" I asked, lifting my head. "Lea, do you know where Erick, Joost, Mordecai, and Cristo are?"

"I contacted them on their com stones when you were checking on the list of members in Cypress," she said. "Erick and Joost are in California. They confirmed that the world is frozen over there as well, and that the Primas in those two towns are missing. Mordecai was on his way to the town in Texas, and Cristo was heading to

Oregon. They said they'd let me know what they found, but that the world was frozen in darkness everywhere they'd been to so far."

"So we at least can assume the entire United States is affected," I said, my hands starting to tremble. "Possibly the world. That means we're dealing with someone powerful and evil enough to cast a spell capable of stopping time indefinitely. That kind of dark magic has to involve human sacrifice. I can't even imagine how many deaths it took to cast the spell. We have no idea what they want or how long they intend to keep us in darkness, but we know she's going to continue to kill someone for every hour the spell is maintained."

"What's our next step?" Jackson asked.

I took a moment, listening to the sound of my breath go in and out. I kept thinking there must be someone else who could make these decisions and lead us in the right direction, but they were all looking to me. What if I chose wrong? What if my decisions put us all in more danger?

I longed for my father.

"We try to figure out what the hell this priestess wants from us. Someone needs to go after the hunter," I said, finally. I knew Jackson wouldn't be happy with it, but there was only one person who could track her and hope to come back alive.

Lea stood and nodded, understanding what I was asking before I even said the words. "I'll go," she said.

Aerden moved to stand, but then sat back down again. Worry crossed his features.

"I'm good at tracking hunters," she said. "I'll leave right away."

I nodded. "Thank you. Make sure you take one of the ruby com stones so you can keep us updated on where you are," I said. "If you find her, see if she'll lead you to whoever she's working for. Anything you can find out about what those hunters were after inside the dome is going to be important to us now. It's no coincidence these attacks happened on the same night, and we need to know why they were there. I think it was more than just revenge. This witch has an agenda."

"Essex and I will go to Venom," Mary Anne said. "We'll fly up to Chicago now that the entrance has been fixed."

"Why Venom?" I asked.

"Well, I'm guessing the priestess's spell didn't affect us because we were outside the boundaries of this world at the time. If that's true, there's a chance everyone who was at Venom last night is unaffected, too. The club exists in a space between worlds, doesn't it?"

"Great idea," I said. "And if he's okay, Rend might be able to help us gather information. A lot of demons and witches pass through Venom on a weekly basis. Maybe he overheard something strange or knows someone who can help us figure out how to get the world running again."

"Just be careful," Jackson said. "I don't like the idea of us splitting up for too long. It makes us more vulnerable."

"What should I tell Mordecai and the guys?" Lea asked. "Should they come back here?"

"Yes, have them come back here when they're done checking out those other towns," I said. "With the world the way it is, they should be able to fly in demon form without any problems. We may need them soon."

She nodded and left to go pack her things.

"You should try to get some rest," Jackson said, reaching over to take my hand.

"How can I possibly sleep with Eloise and Caroline missing?" I asked. "More than three thousand witches gone because they agreed to help us? Every hour we don't figure this out, someone else dies. It's all my fault, Jackson. I'm the one who put them in danger."

"We were all a part of it, Harper," he said. "And those witches knew what they were getting into when they joined with us."

"Not all of them," I said, the tears beginning to fall now. "They took the children, too, Jackson. Those little girls have no idea what the Order even is, much less which side they'd be on if they knew. They're innocents, and God knows what that witch is doing to them right now."

I began to cry and Jackson wrapped his arms around me. Mary Anne stood and placed a hand on my shoulder.

"We all knew the risks we were taking when we started this fight," she said. "We just have to find out where this witch is keeping them and go kick her ass."

I laughed despite my tears and wiped the wetness from my cheeks.

"This witch is more dangerous than we knew," I said. "Maybe Priestess Winter wasn't as strong as some of her other sisters. Or maybe they're working together this time. All I know is that a spell powerful enough to stop time across the entire globe is beyond my comprehension. It terrifies me."

"We have something stronger than that," Jackson said, standing and pulling me into his arms.

"What?" I asked.

He smiled down at me and wiped more tears from my eyes.

"We have each other."

Sarra Cannon

The Memory Of His Warmth

Lea

Fear and doubt rolled through my veins like a toxic tide.

Ever since those tense moments at the Cypress Prima's house, my heart had been pounding. I'd been struggling to stay calm during the meeting, but now that I was alone in the privacy of my own room, the panic was starting to seep in. I couldn't stand still. I couldn't even think straight.

What the hell was going on?

I knew it was possible to lock the memories of objects or places. Hell, I'd done it myself a dozen times. But I'd never once come across a memory locked by someone else.

And there was only one demon I knew who had the ability other than myself.

But what would he have been doing in Cypress? As far as I knew, my father had never even been to the human world. From what Andros had told me, my father hadn't left the King's City in decades.

When I was a little girl, he used to venture out to the villages to check on his subjects and resolve disputes. He'd even taken joy in those trips, always telling me that it was a king's duty to know what was going on in even the farthest corner of his kingdom.

The stronger the Order became, though, the less he left the safety of his castle. If any of the villagers needed to see the king for any reason, they had to travel to the castle and request a meeting with him. After Aerden's disappearance, he had stopped handling a lot of the business of the kingdom directly, passing the responsibility to his council members.

I hadn't been home to the castle or even set foot in the King's City in more than thirty years, and in that time, many said the king had become reclusive and mysterious, rarely making appearances. It got worse each year, which was part of the reason Andros and the higher members of the Resistance had become so desperate for me to stand up against my father.

But Andros didn't know what he was asking of me. My father may not be the demon he used to be, but he was still my king. He had been the ruler of the Northern Kingdom for more than six hundred years. Ripping that control from him would not be easy. And worse, it would be treason.

A betrayal of the worst kind.

In our kingdom, no king had ever been overthrown. They were left to rule as they saw fit until the time came when they decided to pass the crown to their oldest child.

But if the rumors were true and my father had brought a stone guardian to the city, there might be no other choice. Especially if he'd had anything to do with the attacks against us tonight.

Who else could have possibly locked that memory in darkness?

I closed my eyes and leaned against the wooden frame of my closet door.

I had a lot of decisions to make. Once I tracked down this hunter and found out what she knew, I would have to decide whether to come back here to be a part of the fight or to join Andros and the Resistance in a fight against my father.

I took a deep breath and straightened my shoulders.

I didn't have time to be scared. I had to follow my heart above all, and my heart was telling me that I belonged in the Shadow World. I may have abandoned my father, and he may have abandoned his people, but I needed to show the demons of the

Northern Kingdom that I had not abandoned them. I believed in what Harper and the Demon Liberation Movement were doing here in the human world, but I had a duty as heir to the throne in the Northern Kingdom.

Besides, if we were successful in bringing him down, I would have a lot more power to help the Demon Liberation Movement as Queen of the North than I would ever have as a mere princess.

I clenched my jaw and grabbed the small backpack from the bottom of my closet. I stuffed a handful of shirts and an extra pair of black leather pants inside. I didn't have room to take much, but all I really needed was a few changes of clothes and my weapons.

I set the pack on my bed and went into the bathroom to take a shower. I left the water cold, the freezing temperature clearing my head and helping me focus on the journey I was about to take.

When I got out, I dressed and put my hair into one long braid that reached all the way down my back.

The door to my room creaked as it opened. Aerden set his own leather backpack on the bed next to mine. "I'm coming with you," he said.

I sighed and pointed. "Close the door."

He shut it and walked toward me. "I'm not going to argue about this, Lea," he said. "I'm not going to let you go alone."

I studied his face. He wasn't joking around, and I knew telling him to stay here was pointless. At the same time, I had already decided I wouldn't be coming back here. I had no idea what kind of battle awaited me back home, and I didn't want to put him in any danger, especially if my father did have a stone guardian protecting him.

"I can handle this myself."

His blue eyes sparked and a slight smile teased his lips. "I don't doubt that," he said. "But you shouldn't have to face this alone. I know you're holding information back on purpose. I don't completely understand why, but if the enemy we're facing is greater than just one priestess in the Order, you're going to need me."

I looked away and fiddled with my bag. I hadn't let Harper and the others know the full extent of what had happened, because I didn't want anyone to jump to conclusions. I wanted to find out what truly happened before anyone started accusing my father of being involved.

"Aerden, listen, this is something I need to do on my own," I said. "I have no idea what I'm going to find, but if it's at all what I suspect or fear, this is going to be a very dangerous trip for anyone involved."

"All the more reason for me to come with you," he said. "I know you can handle yourself, but it can't hurt to have someone you trust at your side."

"The DLM needs you," I said. "They're going to need everyone helping to investigate each of the cities and rescue the witches who have gone missing. After what Harper and the others did for you, you owe them your loyalty."

I leaned down to retrieve my bow from under the bed. When I stood, Aerden wrapped his hand around my wrist. I lifted my eyes to his, my heart beating too fast.

"The only person I owe my loyalty to is you," he said, his gaze not letting go of me. "You have always been and always will be my princess, Lazalea. I left you once before, but I swear on my life, I will never leave your side again."

His words shook me to my core. It had been a long time since anyone had spoken to me about loyalty with such passion in their eyes. I couldn't quite catch my breath.

"Aerden, I know you've been avoiding going back home," I said, my mouth dry. "I don't want to cause you any more pain."

"I can handle it," he said. "I can't avoid my homeland forever. I need to face what happened all those years ago. It's time."

"Are you sure?" I asked, my voice wavering.

"I'm sure," he said, his eyes locked on mine. "And no matter what you're afraid we might find once we're there, I want to be by your side when you face it."

I nodded. His hand still gripped my wrist and his skin was warm against mine, distracting me. These days I avoided touch, acting as if there was a barrier around me, the same way I had placed a wall around my heart. If I didn't touch anyone or let them close to me, there was little chance they would get into my heart the way I had once let Jackson into my heart.

But the constant pressure and warmth of his touch both excited and calmed me in ways I hadn't felt in a very long time. The weight of his words and commitment gave me courage, and I knew in my soul that he was right. I did need him.

"Jackson's going to be pissed," I said, letting a smile spread slowly across my face.

Aerden smiled back, and even though he finally released his grip on my wrist, the memory of his warmth stayed with me for a long time.

Only A Matter Of Time

Jackson

I stood outside Lea's room for a moment before I knocked. I could hear voices inside and knew Aerden had followed her in there, but I was afraid to knock on the door. I knew what was coming, and I didn't want to face it.

But I had seen the look on Lea's face throughout the meeting downstairs. Something inside her had shifted over the past few days, and even though I wasn't sure of the details, I knew the end result. She was leaving us, and part of me wondered if she ever intended on coming back.

I guess if I was honest with myself, I had always known it was only a matter of time. In a way, I was surprised she had stuck around here as long as she had.

The only reason Lea had come to the human world was to be with me. I had come to rescue Aerden, but like everyone else, Lea had no real hope that we would ever be able to free him. She had come here to try to resurrect what she thought we once had, and I'd been too afraid to tell her it was never real.

Aerden was the one who had always loved her. The heart stone she opened during our engagement ceremony was not filled with my love. It was his. He knew I didn't love her, and he knew he could never have her. Who she married was a choice that was made by our parents long before we understood it. To spare her the pain of seeing a dim light inside that stone, he had placed his own love inside and disappeared.

She had a right to know that, but it wasn't entirely my secret to tell.

Now that Aerden was free and I was engaged to someone else, Lea had no reason to stay in Peachville. Yes, she agreed to stay and help the Demon Liberation Movement, but I knew her heart was with the demons in the Northern Kingdom.

And I knew my brother's heart was with her.

I finally knocked on her door, the weight of losing them heavy on my shoulders. The voices inside grew quiet.

"Lea?" I said. "Is Aerden in there with you?"

After a long pause, the door opened. Lea had a bag slung across one shoulder and her bow on the other. I could see the truth in her dark eyes and it slammed against my heart.

She stepped aside and lowered her head as Aerden moved forward.

"You won't convince me to stay," he said.

"I'm not even going to try," I said. "But I would like to talk to you before you go."

He and Lea exchanged glances and she nodded. "I'll be downstairs," she said. "Don't be too long. I want to reach the borderlands before nightfall."

She left and closed the door behind her.

"She'll make a great queen someday if she wants it," I said after a few moments of tense silence.

"She's so different now than the girl I remember."

The sadness in his voice made my heart tighten. He blamed me for that, and with good reason. Lea had loved me for our entire lives, and I had broken her heart.

But what Aerden never understood was that he broke mine first.

"We've all changed," I said. "We've been through a lot."

My words hung between us, and I knew it was so much more complex than that.

162

Yes, we'd been through a lot, but none of us more than Aerden. He'd been a slave to the Order and to Peachville's Prima line for a hundred years. I couldn't even begin to imagine what that must have been like for him. Any time I tried to talk to him about it or get him to open up about his feelings since he'd been set free, he shut me out.

He was so full of anger and regret and rage that the demon I'd known as my twin brother had all but disappeared inside that tangle of emotions. I wanted nothing more than to bring him back from the dead, but how do you resurrect someone who won't even speak to you? Sometimes he acted like his freedom was more of a burden than a gift.

Standing here, knowing he was about to leave, I wished I had the words to finally break through to him. To let him know how much I loved him.

But there was this wall between us that I couldn't seem to get past.

I wanted to explain to him about all that had happened when he was stolen from us. I wanted to tell him I'd gone mad when he left, and that I couldn't possibly have followed through on my promise to take care of Lea. Not with him being tortured and used by the Order.

I wanted him to understand that my love for him was far greater than anything I'd ever felt for another one of our kind. But how could I say all that? There were too many words still to say. Too much time that had gone by.

And now we were being separated again. My heart almost couldn't take it.

When I finally lifted my eyes to him, he was staring out the window toward the back of the house. I joined him there and saw Lea in the garden, her dark braid falling down her back as she checked for something in her backpack.

"Why don't you tell her how you feel?" I asked quietly, well aware of the fact I was stepping on a minefield. "Now that I've given Harper my heart stone, don't you think it's time Lea knew the truth about the one I gave her all those years ago?"

Aerden's eyes closed and turned away.

"She deserves to know the truth."

"It's too late for that," he said.

"It's never too late for true love," I said.

"You're wrong." The anger I'd become so used to hearing in his voice bellowed back at me. "Yes, I loved her once, but she was never meant for me. She never loved me even half as much as she loved you. And she never will. Telling her the truth now would only hurt her more."

"How can you know that?" I asked. "Neither one of us knows what might have happened if you hadn't left that day. What if you had told her the truth instead of walking away? When I asked her for the stone back on Halloween night, do you know what she said to me?"

Tears pushed at the edges of my eyes.

Aerden glanced at me and shook his head.

"She told me that seeing that bright light inside the heart stone was the happiest moment of her life. Knowing someone loved her that much was her greatest joy. Now she thinks that love was a lie, but it wasn't. It was real, Aerden. She just doesn't know that it was you."

He turned away from me, but I walked over and put my hand on his shoulder, spinning him back toward me. "If you had told her how you felt back then, that the love inside the stone was yours and not mine, how can you know she wouldn't have chosen you instead?"

He yanked away and put up his hand to warn me to stay back.

"I made a mistake when I poured my own love into that stone," he said. "I realize that now. Your engagement to her was going to happen no matter what any of us wanted, even Lea."

"She didn't deserve to be lied to," I said. "I never should have gone along with it."

"What you should have done was follow through," he shouted, pressing a finger hard into my chest. He took several shallow breaths and then backed away. "You should have let me go. The two of you would have been married by now, and Lea would have been happy."

"How can you still believe that after all this time?" I asked him. "After everything you've seen and experienced, can you honestly tell me that you think anyone is happier when they're living a lie? When they're forced to live the life someone else decided they should live?"

Aerden's face crumpled and his jaw clenched. He balled his hands into tight fists and lowered his head. A tear rolled down his cheek. He started to turn away, but I grabbed his arm and turned him back to me, not letting go.

"We can't change the past. What's done is done, Aerden. All we can do is try to move forward the best we can," I said. "I'm sorry I couldn't make her happy, but I loved you more. Like it or not, you are a piece of me, and I couldn't abandon you. I would rather be dead than live knowing you were being tortured by the Order."

He pulled his arm from my grasp and placed his fist against the wall, leaning forward against it.

"And I would never have been happy married to Lea," I said. "Obeying every command our parents gave us. Trust me when I tell you that she wouldn't have been happy either, Aerden. No matter how much you try to convince yourself she would have. She would have lived her life knowing something was standing between us. Your heart was in the right place, but letting her believe the love inside that stone belonged to me has hurt her more than anything."

I moved closer to him. I didn't want to argue. I just wanted him to understand. To open up.

"Aerden, I don't want you to go, but I understand why you need to follow her," I said. "I need you to forgive me for coming after you and abandoning Lea. I need you to tell me you understand why I did what I did. There's been a wall between us ever since you went free, and before you leave here, I need to know we're okay. That we're still brothers."

He turned, tears shining in his eyes, his lower lip trembling with tension.

"I don't know what you expect from me," he said.

"I just need some kind of sign that my brother is still in there somewhere," I said in a whisper, barely able to hold back my own tears. "I need to know you're going to be okay."

He shook his head and backed away. He grabbed his bag from the bed and opened the door.

"You should have let me go," he said. "I love you, Jackson, but you should have just let me go."

He stepped through the door and with each sound of his footsteps on the stairs, my heart broke just a little more.

I'm Ready

Aerden

I hesitated at the bottom of the stairs and glanced back toward Lea's room.

I knew I was being a jerk to my own brother, but it was too hard to face it all. I pushed back tears. I refused to let those emotions rise to the surface, because whatever sorrow was locked deep inside terrified me.

I was afraid that if I ever started talking about it, the pain would swallow me whole.

I hated myself for the brisk tone I had taken with him.

He was my twin brother, after all. The only family I had left who gave a damn about me. He deserved better.

I cleared my throat and hiked my bag higher on my shoulder. I desperately wished I could find the words to tell him I understood what he had done for me. I may have been angry with him for abandoning the Shadow World and for leaving Lea behind, but I also knew he had sacrificed all of that for me. I wanted him to know how much it meant that he had risked his life to save me when everyone else had given up hope.

But I wasn't ready.

The pain was still too raw, and the rage I felt every time I thought about the Order and what they had taken from me was sometimes the only thing keeping me alive.

The anger was easier to feel than the pain of regret.

Someday, I hoped I would have the courage to tell Jackson about those years I spent in slavery, and how grateful I was that he'd saved me. But there was a part of me that believed everyone would have been better off if they'd simply forgotten I existed. He would have married Lea and taken the throne. They might have been happy together. Safe.

His words echoed in my head, but I pushed them out. I needed to hold onto what I believed, because anything else was just too scary to face right now.

Lea met me on the front porch.

"You sure you're up for this?" she asked. "A lot has changed about our world since you were last in the north."

A shudder ran down my spine. I was willing to follow Lea wherever she needed to go, but I'd be lying if I said I wasn't nervous about going home for the first time in what felt like forever.

"I'm fine," I said, sounding more sure than I really felt.

Everyone joined us outside to say goodbye.

I held onto Jackson for a long moment, feeling the weight of words I couldn't say between us. "I'll see you in this world or the next, my brother," I said.

"Come home soon," he said, his eyes filling with tears.

Lea and I made our way through the gardens and past the old shed. When we reached the edge of the woods, I turned and glanced back at the house, not knowing if it would be weeks or years before we would return, but hoping that someday, I would see it again.

I felt a strange attachment to this place. Some of the others had been living here for a few months or years, but I had been living on this estate for over a hundred years. Even though I'd been brought here against my will, this had become my home.

I had no idea what to expect on the other side. I wasn't the same demon I was a hundred years ago, and from what I'd heard, the

Shadow World had endured great change as well. I'd been to Harper's domed city a few times, but I hadn't been back to my true homeland in the north since the day I was taken.

But it was time. I'd avoided facing the truth for way too long. It was time to venture out and see if I still had what it took to be a real warrior after all these years.

"You sure you're okay?" Lea asked.

"I'm ready," I said.

"Come on." She touched my shoulder. "We have a long journey ahead of us."

I nodded and followed her into the woods, toward the patch of white roses along the banks of Brighton Lake—our portal from this world to the place of my ancestors, where my past awaited.

Sarra Cannon

It's Happening To Me

Harper

The house felt so quiet and empty. Mary Anne and Essex left for Chicago shortly after Lea and Aerden made their way to the Shadow World. Courtney was sitting upstairs with Sophie, trying to restore the girl's power, but she was having a difficult time. Courtney was great at restoring power when a witch had used it organically, but when power was stolen using dark magic, it could be much more difficult to bring it back.

I just hoped it wasn't impossible.

Guilt gnawed at me. I was the one who had brought Sophie back to stay with Eloise in Cypress. After losing her family, there was nowhere else to go where she would be safe, but I hadn't realized just how dangerous Cypress might be for her.

The fact that the emerald priestess had used the poor girl to bring a message to me broke my heart. It wasn't fair. Sophie had done nothing to deserve such torture.

I prayed she would be okay.

I'd been pacing the room as Courtney tried to heal the girl's power, but Courtney had eventually asked me to leave, saying my emotions were interfering with her concentration.

So I had come downstairs to the kitchen to make coffee.

It should have been morning by now. The sun should have been coming up and the group should have been gathered here in the kitchen for breakfast.

Instead, it was pitch black out there, the world locked in the darkness of the spell.

I sat down at the table with my coffee and tried to think through our next steps. The first thing we needed to do was figure out what reasons the emerald priestess would have for freezing the world at three in the morning. I'd learned early on in my time here in Peachville that three was a special time for the Order. It was when they performed all of their initiation ceremonies and when every portal had been created. There was something magical about it, and it was believed this was the time of night when the link between our world and the Shadow World was at its most powerful.

But if the entire world was frozen at this time, wouldn't it still only be midnight on the West Coast? That meant whatever the priestess had planned, she was close.

Jackson walked into the kitchen and sat down next to me.

"How are you holding up?" I asked.

He shrugged and set his elbows against the table. "I can't believe he's gone," he said. "I guess I knew I couldn't keep the group together forever, but I expected him to be here with me for years, at the very least."

I put my hand on his wrist and squeezed. We were all being separated from those we loved right now, and that was one of the hardest things in the world to endure, especially when you had no idea whether those people would ever find their way back to you.

"Do you want some coffee?"

He nodded and I turned slightly in my chair, concentrating on a cup I'd set out for him on the counter. I poured the coffee, stirred in a little cream and sugar, and floated the cup over to us.

He gave a small smile and wrapped his hands around the warm mug. "I keep forgetting you can do that," he said. "You're getting so good at psychokinesis. I remember when you could barely move one thing at a time, and that was only when you were angry."

172

"Practice makes perfect," I said, trying to be funny, but it came out flat.

"Hopefully they'll find that hunter and be back soon," he said. "But I get the feeling Lea's got other plans."

I studied him, my eyes wide. "What do you mean?"

"You can't tell me you haven't noticed her becoming more withdrawn lately?"

I shrugged. "I noticed, but that's only natural considering what's been happening between you and me."

"We couldn't very well expect her to live here with us after we got engaged, I guess," he said. "But I hoped she would find a way to deal with it. I don't know. I can't help but wonder if there's something more going on with her than we know."

"Like what?" I asked.

"I wish I knew," he said. "But I've been friends with Lea for a long time—over two hundred years—and I'm pretty sure she's been keeping something from us."

I groaned and put my head in my hands. It felt like one bad thing after another. If people on our own team were keeping secrets, how were we ever going to defeat the Order?

"We're having a bad couple of days," Jackson said with a laugh.

"You think?" I raised my head and couldn't help but smile. I was so grateful to have him here with me now.

"Let's talk this through, then," he said. "Who? And why? Those are the main questions that need to be answered right now."

"Well, we have a good idea of the who," I said.

"But we can't be sure the attack on the Southern Kingdom is the same person."

"No, but it would be a crazy coincidence for them both to happen on the same night if it were two different enemies, right? Even if it's two different sisters attacking us, the timing is too close together for it not to be coordinated."

"Good point," he said. "There was something else that was odd about the attack in the Shadow World, too."

"What?"

"First of all, none of the hunters who died left any kind of talisman," he said. "Every time we've ever killed a hunter, they've had something on them that tells us which sister they belong to, right? A ring or a pendant of some kind. A summoning stone. But none of them were carrying one."

"None of the ones we killed, anyway," I said. "There's still a chance the one Lea and Aerden are tracking down will have something on her."

"Yes, but there's more," he said. "I recognized one of those hunters. When I couldn't find Lea on the battlefield, I went looking for her. She was up in the trees fighting, and she believes that hunter was the one who'd been casting the shields and also bringing down the dome with her magic. She was incredibly powerful, and I would say she must have had some kind of special abilities with shields or barriers, which was why she was hiding where the rest of our guards couldn't see her."

"You knew her?"

"Harper, it was Mayor Chen, Lark's mom," he said. "I'm sure of it."

My mouth fell open. "Oh my God," she said. "That means someone turned her into a hunter after Priestess Winter died. She was here that day, fighting against us."

He shook his head. "Who would have done that? And why? She was loyal to the Order."

My ears started to ring and my blood pumped harder. "The same thing happened to Zara's aunt," I said. "She was obviously loyal to the Order, but she'd been turned into a hunter, anyway."

"Exactly," he said. "Which is part of what's strange about that attack. We don't have any real evidence about which priestess they were sent by today, but if two of them were part of the Winter family—"

"I think it's happening to me, too," Zara said.

I hadn't heard her come in, and I jumped when she spoke. She stood in the hallway just beyond the entrance to the kitchen, her normal happy smile missing from her pale face. Something was definitely happening to her.

With all the fighting, I'd pushed it from my mind, not wanting to deal with it, but looking at her now, it was shocking how fast she was changing.

Her hair was mostly black, brittle and dull at the ends. Her skin had become almost translucent, thick black veins running across her hands.

"Zara, what's going on?" I asked. I glanced at the chair next to Jackson and it slid backward across the floor. I stood and helped her to the chair. "What's happening to you?"

She sat down, her head lowered. "I keep thinking about her," she said. "I keep seeing her face over and over in my mind. The way she smiled when she saw me, like she was surprised and happy to see me or something. And the way she touched my hair."

She began to cry.

"I don't understand," I said, my heart aching. "Why are you changing like this?"

"I think I'm turning into one of them," she said through her sobs. "A hunter. I don't know when it started, but it's happening really fast, Harper. I'm scared."

I felt like the breath had been knocked out of me. My skin tingled and my heart tightened.

"Zara, that can't be it," I said, not wanting to believe it. "We can reverse it. We're going to figure this out."

"My body is growing weaker by the minute," she said. "I wasn't sure what was going on, but when I heard Jackson say Mayor Chen was one of the other hunters, I just knew. I think that somehow, all of my mother's bloodline is changing into them."

"Why?" I asked, knowing no one had an answer. "Why would that happen?"

"A priestess of the Order has never died before," Jackson said. "We never really considered the consequences that might have on her family line."

"But why now?" I asked. "Why not six months ago? I don't understand."

Panic shot through me. How long did she have?

We needed to do something that would give us answers, instead of sitting around making guesses.

"Lea's already searching for the hunter, your Aunt Mindy," I said. "Maybe finding her will give us some answers. What else can we do?"

"I'll contact Mary Anne," Jackson said. "Maybe Rend has some kind of potion that can reverse this."

He got up from the table and went into the next room to activate one of the communication stones he'd sent with them.

Zara lifted her head, her black hair falling around her face. "The iron cage," she said. "It's the only real clue."

I nodded. "Yes, but that's not going to tell us how to save you."

"It gives us a starting point," she said.

I didn't understand what she meant. How would the cages give us a starting point?

Zara stood, pushing her chair back. "You said you had seen cages like that before in the basement of my mother's house, right?"

"Yes, but—"

"Then that's where we need to start," she said. Fear made her lip tremble. "We need to go back to Winterhaven."

Dust In My Hands

Harper

Zara and I decided to go alone.

Jackson didn't like the idea of us going back to that evil place without him, but he agreed that there wasn't much of a choice. We couldn't leave Courtney and Sophie here alone to defend Brighton Manor, and we needed someone here in case there was another attack.

"We'll be okay," I said, wrapping my arms around him. I lay my head against his chest and took a few deep breaths, enjoying the warmth of him. "We're just going to see if the cage actually came from the basement or if it was just another cage that looks similar."

"I don't see what kind of answers this is going to give us," he said.

"It will at least tell us if someone else has been there inside the house," I said. "Maybe they left some kind of clue behind."

"That still won't tell us what the emerald priestess is after," he said. "And it's dangerous to be going back there."

"Every move we make right now is going to be dangerous," I said.

"You're weak, Harper. You've been through a lot in the past twenty-four hours. You need to rest. And Zara—"

"Right now, Zara needs us to do everything we can to try to save her. Maybe there's something in her mother's library that will tell us how to reverse the spell. What else can we do? We can't just sit here. Besides, how could I possibly rest knowing Eloise and her daughter are trapped somewhere?" I asked. "You know me better than that."

His arms tightened around me, holding on as long as he could.

Zara joined us in the upstairs hallway. "I'm ready," she said. She'd changed clothes and gotten the butterfly pendant she'd given me from my room. She opened it and stuck the pin through the fabric of my black cotton tank top. "This should allow you to get inside and move around in there in case we get separated."

"Be careful," Jackson said.

"We will, I promise," I said. I stood on my tiptoes and kissed him. "I love you."

"I love you, too. I'll see you soon," he said. "You have a communication stone?"

I pulled it out of my pocket and held the ruby up for him to see.

He let out a nervous breath and nodded.

Zara and I ascended the narrow steps to the attic and paused inside the pentagram-shaped room at the top.

"I'm sorry you have to do this," I said. "I know you haven't been back there much."

She took a deep breath and raised her shoulders. "It's going to be fine," she said. "Besides, this will give me a chance to grab those cute pink shoes I forgot to get last time I was there."

She laughed, but it was no longer the singsong giggle of a child. There was a darkness inside her laughter now.

"Let's go," I said, panic fueling my footsteps. We had to do something. I couldn't lose her, too.

I opened the door with a demon face carved into the front and walked into the Hall of Doorways. After avoiding this corridor for months, it was strange to be back inside twice on the same day.

We made our way through, Zara holding up an orb of glowing pink light to illuminate the symbols on the doorways. When we found the blue butterfly on the Winters' door, she bit her lower lip and sighed.

"Here we are," she said. "Home sweet home."

I reached for her hand and held it tightly as I opened the door to her old house.

It creaked as it opened, the sound echoing through the hallway. The room inside was dark and cold. With no one living at Winterhaven, there was no one to turn on the heat in the winter months. I shivered and sat down in the center of the room.

"What are you doing?" she whispered.

"I'm going to explore as far as I can with my mind before we go down there," I said. "Just in case someone's already set up camp here or set some kind of trap for us. If I can, I'm going to try to get all the way to the basement room with the cages and see if I can tell if one is missing. If I can manage it, maybe we won't have to go down there at all."

"I didn't know you could do that," she said. "How does it work?"

"It's something I learned when I was hiding out in the Underground," I said. "If I focus, I can sort of walk around and see what's going on without actually being there in physical form."

"Astral projection," she said. "I've heard of it, but never actually known someone who could do it."

"It takes a lot out of me, but we can't afford to take any risks right now."

She nodded and glanced at the library door. "I'm going to see if I can find anything about what's happening to me in my mother's library," she said. "I'll meet you back here when you're done."

I crossed my legs underneath my body and put my palms on my knees. I closed my eyes and took several deep breaths, trying to shut out all my fear and worry, and focus only on the house itself.

After a few moments, I separated my mind from my physical body and floated down the stairs to the second floor. In this state, I couldn't see colors and objects with complete clarity, but I could get a basic image of what everything looked like.

The doors to the many bedrooms on the second floor of the house were open, and after a quick glance inside, I didn't see anything that looked out of place. I'd never been inside Priestess

Winter's bedroom, but when I came across the only closed door on the hall, I somehow knew it had been hers.

I couldn't open doors in this disembodied state, but I could pass through them like a ghost.

I entered her bedroom, shivering at the overwhelming feeling of being cold, even though my body was still on the third floor.

The room was decorated in harsh bright whites and icy blues, the bed perfectly made. A crystal vase on the table held flowers that had long since withered and died. If I could have touched them, they would have fallen to dust in my hands.

I searched for any sign of a jewelry box, thinking that if I was an intruder or even a family member looking for valuables, that would be the first place I'd look. Any gemstones in this witch's jewelry box could contain magical spells or abilities most humans wouldn't know to look for. But after a couple of minutes of searching, I couldn't find any jewelry at all.

Something struck me as I thought about the sapphire butterfly pinned to my shirt. A strange nagging thought I couldn't quite place.

Why had Sophie had an emerald pendant in her jewelry box in Cypress?

She had grown up in a sapphire gate, not an emerald one. The scarab pendant could have been a gift from Eloise to welcome her to the emerald gates, but still, something about it disturbed me.

Not wanting to waste any more time, I made my way back through the door and down the hall to the grand staircase that led to the first floor.

One of the most powerful things about being in this ethereal form was that I could sense energy, especially if that energy was coming from another person. As I passed through the beautifully opulent rooms on the main floor, I searched for that energy. I was looking for any sign of life at all inside the house, but it felt empty and freezing cold, as if no one had been here for a very long time.

I made my way to the kitchen and took a deep breath as I sent my energy down the hidden staircase to the basement.

Down a short hallway, I came to the ritual room. It was empty, just like the rest of the house. I stared down at the sapphire embedded in the floor. This was where it all began. This was the very first portal ever created, and it gave me a sense of satisfaction to see a long crack down the middle, a result of Priestess Winter's death.

I pushed my energy down the hallway toward the room with the cages. The first time I was down here, there was a narrow wooden door closing it off from the rest of the house, but now, the door was completely gone, removed from its hinges, leaving a dark chasm of space.

I walked into the darkness, wishing there was some way to cast an orb of light down there, but as far as I knew, it was impossible to be more than an observer when I was exploring an area with my mind.

Goose bumps broke out along my skin as I stepped into the room and looked up the rows of iron cages hanging above me. The last time I had been here, I found my own sister trapped inside, the life draining from her body.

There had been twenty cages back then, filled with witches and other people who had somehow wronged Priestess Winter. I counted them now, and knew without a doubt that someone had been here.

Only seventeen cages hung from the ceiling, and I shivered. One of the missing cages was in Sophie's room in Cypress. But where were the other two? And who did they plan to keep inside?

Just before I pulled my mind back to my body, I felt a tingle along my spine. An energy that hadn't been there before.

When I turned back toward the cages, I saw the shadow of a woman in dark cloak inside the nearest one, the hood pulled over her head to hide her face.

I pushed my mind upward, frantic. Was this the woman from my dreams? Why was she here?

But when I reached the iron cage, she was gone. There was no trace of her inside.

I quickly forced my mind back to the attic, anxious to tell Zara what I had seen. I wanted to run downstairs to see if we could find the cloaked woman. Had she been here? What was her part in all this?

But when my eyes snapped open in the pentagram-shaped room on the third floor, I was alone.

I stood and searched for Zara, calling her name. I opened the door to the library, and found her sitting on the floor, tears falling like rain against her cheeks.

A small book was cradled against her chest, and when I went to her, she handed it to me, her finger holding the book open to a page toward the end.

"What's this?" I asked.

"My mother's journal," she said. "Read it."

My eyes dipped to the passage Zara pointed to.

And if any of you, my lovely daughters, are reading this now when I am gone, know this. If I'm dead, it's because you either failed to protect me, or you betrayed me. Now, you will know what betrayal feels like. You'll see it in the way your hair changes color and begins to decay. You will know it when you look at your face in the mirror.

If I cannot rule, I will not allow one of you, the ungrateful, to rule in my place.

I have placed a curse on my own bloodline, which will activate shortly after my death. It will affect the oldest of my daughters first, following through, in time, to the youngest. You will become what all witches who've betrayed me have become. Hunters. You will live forever, and your decaying body will serve as a constant reminder of what you did to me.

There is no cure. There is no way out.

Accept your fate as you watch your life slip through your hands, for you brought this on yourself.

I lowered the journal and grabbed Zara's hand, unable to hold back my tears. When I killed Priestess Winter, I never imagined she would be able to reach out from the grave and continue to spread such evil.

Hopelessness overwhelmed me, and I pulled my dear friend into my arms.

There were no words to say. There was only this moment to let her know how much I loved her.

He's All That Matters To Me

Aerden

The heat of six suns beat down on us as we traveled through the Southern Kingdom toward the borderlands. Lea and I traveled in shadow form for a while, through the forests and across the grassy plains, but when we lost the trail of the hunter's magic, we took solid form and traveled on foot.

Lea was good at tracking. I remembered that from when we were younger. It was something I had been trained in as a shadowling, but I had forgotten most of what I'd been taught. I was impressed with the way she was able to quickly pull up a spark of memory from a place and easily see which way the hunter had gone.

The more traditional way of tracking was to follow the path of someone's magic. Most beings who traveled here in the Shadow World used magic in some way, either shifting to a shadowed form or using speed spells. The distances between cities could sometimes take days to travel on foot, and since we didn't use cars like they had in the human world, most demons used magic.

But magic was relatively easy to track, if you knew what you were looking for.

Lea knelt low to the ground and stared ahead, studying the ground and the air just above it.

"She went this way," she said. "Toward the borderlands."

"How did you know she would go this way?" I asked.

"What do you mean?"

"Earlier, when we were back at Brighton Manor, you said you wanted to reach the borderlands by nightfall. How did you know we'd be going this way?"

"I didn't," she said. "Not for sure, anyway. But most hunters have no reason to be in the south anymore. When Harper's father built the domed city, he invited everyone who lived in the entire Southern Kingdom to move their families there. He said it was the only way he could protect them from the Order. Villages spread out across the countryside were much harder to patrol and protect than one single city."

"It makes sense," I said.

"He was a wise king," she said. "Unlike my father, who built walls around himself and locked everyone else out."

Her tone was thick with bitterness.

"A few villagers refused to live in the domed city, not wanting to leave their homes," she said. "The hunters came for them first, but eventually, there were too few demons left unprotected here in the south, so all the hunters who used to live on this side of the border went north."

I swallowed, understanding now why she was so angry and sad.

"North, where the villages were left unprotected," I said.

"Yes." She stared at the swampy land that made up the borderlands between the kingdoms. "Aerden, when we cross over to our old homeland, you need to prepare yourself for what you're going to see."

I followed her gaze, my skin growing hot.

"It's nothing like it used to be," she said. "It shocks me every time I come back, just how much our homeland has been pillaged and destroyed by the Order. It's a lot to take in."

"I need to see it," I said. "I can't hide from this forever."

She nodded and began to walk across the swamp. She chose each step carefully, finding solid footing on rocks or upraised moss. It took nearly two hours for us to make our way across less than a mile of swamp, but when we came through the other side, we quickly made our way to the stone wall that separated north from south.

The suns were already making their descent across the sky, joined by two moons already showing through the purple sky to the east.

"There's a crossing about a mile from here," she said. "We'll make our way along the wall until we can cross the bridge to the Northern Kingdom. The suns should be mostly set by then. We'll see if we can make camp somewhere just north of the wall."

"Why not just shift and fly over it?" I asked. "No one's following us or tracking us."

"Not that we know of," she said. "But I don't want to take any risks. The hunter definitely went over the wall here. I can sense her magic strongly in this area, but I'd rather cross at the bridge and double back in the morning. We've been using our own magic up to this point, but from now on, I think we need to be more careful. No more casting unless we have to. I don't want anyone tracking us."

We crossed into the Northern Kingdom just as the suns began to set.

I had never been this far south when I was younger, so I'd never visited any of the borderland villages. Still, as we approached a set of thatched roof houses on the dusty road, my stomach grew nervous and thick with tension.

From a distance, it looked like any small village with a circular arrangement of houses on the outside and a town's center where the market would set up every day. But as we got closer, I noticed holes in the roofs of the houses. Long brown vines had grown up around their exteriors, tangling in the wooden slats.

When we were close enough to see the market at the center of the village, I realized that it was nothing but a bunch of broken stone boxes, filled with rain.

A young woman peered out of the doorway of one of the worn-down homes, a small shadowling hiding behind her skirts. I stepped closer, but she backed away. She had a small sword clasped in her hand.

"We don't have any food," she said. "There's nothing of value here, so whatever you're looking for, you might as well keep going."

I shook my head. "We don't want anything," I said, my heart aching for this woman and her small child. Were they the only ones left here? Why hadn't they moved on? "Where is everyone else?"

She stared at me blankly, as if she hadn't understood my question.

"Where are the rest of the demons in your village?" I asked. "You can't be the only ones left here?"

The child at her knees poked his head around the side of her body and stared at me, his eyes dark and full of curiosity.

"Hi," I said with a smile.

His mother made a hissing sound and the child stepped back behind her, but I could see the glint of a knife in his hand.

I stared at that weapon, clasped in the hand of such a young little thing, wondering what this world had come to when someone so young had to know how to protect themselves because there was no one left to keep them safe.

"Do you need food?" I asked.

"Aerden," Lea said in a hushed voice. "We barely have enough for ourselves to last three days. We can't go giving it out to every weak villager we come across."

I ignored her and stepped closer to the woman in the hut.

I shifted my pack and set it on the ground in front of me. The woman moved backward, her arm outstretched protectively to guard her child.

I held my hands up and shook my head. "I won't hurt you, I promise," I said. "But I have some food in my bag if you'd like some."

The woman's eyes grew wide and her mouth opened. The hunger that pushed through her was like a passionate need. I pulled a protein bar and two apples from my bag and held it toward her.

She leaned her head forward, studying me. But then she gasped and backed away.

"Where did you get that?" she asked. "It doesn't look natural."

I laughed, realizing she meant the wrapped protein bar. "I've been in the human world for a very long time," I said. "It doesn't look good, but it tastes okay, and it's enough to get you through for a little while. Where are the others from your village? Were they all taken?"

She looked down at her feet and then placed a hand on top of her son's head. "Most of them were taken," she said. "Some joined the Resistance, but my family stayed here. It's our home. We didn't know where else to go. A few years ago, my husband was taken. Since then, it's just been the two of us out here. The hunters don't mess with us anymore. Too many villages with more demons to take than here, I guess."

"Have you seen a hunter pass by this way recently?" Lea asked.

The woman looked up at her, as if just now noticing I wasn't alone. Slowly, the woman nodded. "An army of them, headed south. We hid in the cave near the water as they passed, but they didn't seem to care," she said. "They were going after something else."

"Did any of them come back through when they were done?"

"Only one," she said.

Lea and I glanced at each other. "Which way did she go?"

The woman stepped out of her hut and pointed toward the mountains to the west. "She went into those hills," she said. "Why are you asking?"

"Because we want to find her," Lea said.

A pained expression crossed the woman's face. "Why would you go looking for a hunter? That's madness."

"Maybe," Lea said. "But the whole world is madness these days, isn't it?"

The woman smiled and nodded. "Yes, I suppose you're right."

She met my eyes and leaned down to take the food I'd offered. "You sure this stuff is okay to eat?"

I smiled and tilted my head to look again at the small boy inside the hut, his face just peeking out from behind the door. "I promise," I said. "If I can, I'll bring more later."

"Thank you," she said.

I hoisted my backpack on my shoulder and nodded to Lea. She turned toward the mountains and started walking.

"Take care of that boy," I said.

"He's all that matters to me," the woman said, her words tugging at my heart. "And if you're really going toward those mountains, I'd wait until sunrise if I were you. In the dark, the hunters roam those hills in packs."

I nodded and followed Lea through the deserted village and out toward the rocky path that led up toward the mountains.

Something More

Lea

"Let's make camp," I said. I looked to the rocky black mountains just beyond the next hill. We were close, and if I had to guess, the hunter's cave was hidden somewhere close. "We can start up again in the morning."

Aerden set his pack on a large boulder at the edge of a grassy space that looked flat enough to sleep on for the night.

"Don't stop for my sake," he said. "I can keep going if we need to."

I studied him. I knew it had been a rough day for him. It was hard for me to see the destruction and ruin that had come to our lands, but at least I had seen it happen in slow motion, taking it in one year at a time.

He had to see it happen all at once, like waking up after some kind of major apocalypse. Sadly, he hadn't seen the worst of it.

"If we could see in the dark like Jackson, I'd say let's keep going, but neither of us will be any good during the darkest part of the night," I said. "If we use our magic to light the way, the hunter will see us coming and anyone who might be following could track us in an instant. It's safer to rest and start again in the morning."

He nodded and removed his sleeping bag from his pack. I looked around for some firewood in the area. Normally, I'd have had Aerden use his magic to keep us warm. He was naturally gifted with fire, but we'd have to stick to the basics. Luckily, we'd been in the human world long enough to have things like matches and sleeping bags and other comforts that didn't take any magic to use.

I walked a little ways off from the camp and gathered some sticks and twigs to use for the fire.

As the last bit of sunlight disappeared behind the cliffs, I returned to our camp and settled in for the night.

We'd chosen a small alcove at the edge of the mountain, and I hoped no one would be able to see the flames from here. It felt hidden and secluded, something I hadn't had the pleasure of feeling for a long time. Living in a house with a dozen people meant privacy didn't really exist anymore.

And I happened to like privacy.

"What's that smile for?" Aerden asked. "You don't smile enough these days."

I hadn't even realized I was smiling, and warmth rushed to my cheeks.

"It feels good to be out on the land again, fending for myself," I said. "When I first joined the Resistance, we didn't have an underground hideout or anything like that. We lived in the mountains at the very edge of the province. Supplies were sometimes hard to come by, but we made it work. After living in a castle where servants waited on me hand and foot, I kind of liked it, to be honest. I miss that."

I realized as I spoke that I was brushing up against a dangerous topic, but Aerden didn't seem to mind.

He put his dagger through the core of an apple and sliced it into pieces. "Why did you leave the castle?" he asked. "We've never really had the chance to talk about it."

"I always assumed you didn't want to talk about it," I said. "I don't want to say anything that will hurt you or bring back bad memories."

He shrugged, his face hard to read in the firelight. "It all hurts these days, doesn't it? All the memories or thoughts of that time. I'd like to know why you left instead of staying behind and taking your place on the throne."

I sat down next to him on the log of an ash tree he'd pulled over. "I left because Jackson left," I said. "He felt you when you were taken, did you know that?"

Aerden shook his head and looked over at me, waiting for me to say more.

"We were inside the veil, and I had just opened his heart stone," I said. "We were supposed to kiss to seal the promise. I'm sure you know all that, but before we kissed, Jackson collapsed. I didn't understand what was happening, but he was in agony. And then he finally looked up and told me you were dead."

Aerden looked down. "Dead?"

"He said he'd felt you ripped from him, as if you had died," I said. "It wasn't until later that he figured out what had really happened."

"This happened while you were inside the veil? But you did kiss to seal the promise?" he asked.

"Not officially," I said. "I kissed him to bring the veil down so we could get help, but no. Jackson never kissed me. But I saw his heart stone."

I stared into the fire, thinking that even the light from these flames could not compare.

"Seeing that stone was the greatest joy of my life. It surprised me, that light. I've never seen anything so strong and pure in my life, and even though it only lasted a few seconds before it all started to fall apart, there have been times when the joy of looking into that stone and knowing I was loved has sometimes been the only thing that's kept me alive," I said, warm tears pushing to the surface. "I have no idea what made him stop loving me, but it was there, if only for a little while."

Aerden tensed beside me, and I knew I'd probably said too much. The last thing he wanted to do tonight was listen to me complain about losing Jackson. Especially when my pain couldn't compare to what he'd been through.

"Lea," he said, softer than I'd heard him speak for a very long time.

I turned to him and he set his dagger aside. His eyes shone with tears and his chest rose and fell, heavy with each breath. He lifted his hand to my face, his fingers trembling slightly.

I started to move away, not sure what he was doing, but something in his eyes held me there.

His hand reached for the long, dark braid that fell down my back. He pulled it over my shoulder and removed the tie at the end, letting his hands gently untangle each crisscross.

I was speechless, not understanding why he was doing this, but not wanting to move away.

I kept my eyes locked on his face, the firelight flickering across his features. He looked so much like Jackson, but now, I noticed subtle differences I wasn't sure I'd caught before.

The line of his jaw was slightly stronger and more pronounced. A small scar on his forehead above his nose that he'd gotten when we were shadowlings. And when he'd finished taking my hair down, the blue eyes that looked at me were very different from the green eyes of his brother.

These eyes held unimaginable pain behind them, but something more I had never seen in Jackson's eyes. I couldn't define it.

Aerden ran his hand through my hair and pulled it over my shoulder.

"This is how I remember you," he said in a whisper. "Not as a harsh warrior, but as a beautiful princess. You have always been incredibly strong, but you used to have a softness to you that I haven't seen since I went free. I loved that about you."

Chills ran through my body. I looked away, toward the fire, scared to meet his gaze. My heart raced, and I couldn't catch my breath.

Aerden moved to crouch in front of the fire and took my hands in his.

"Lea, there's something I need to tell you about the day I left," he said.

I looked up. It was suddenly as if the world was spinning, and I couldn't get control. What was happening between us? I wasn't sure I wanted this. Over these past few months of training together, we'd somehow naturally gravitated toward each other, always seeking each other out. But I'd thought it was only because we both felt so much pain.

Now, I wasn't so sure.

Panic washed over me like a mountainous wave, threatening to pull me under. I had worked so hard to get control of my pain. I couldn't handle opening myself up to something more.

But as he opened his mouth to speak, something passed close to us. A shadow in the night, its energy filling the air around us.

I snapped my head to the left, recognizing the scent of that magic.

The hunter we'd been searching for was close.

I pulled my hands from his and quickly threw my blanket over the fire, extinguishing the flames. I held a finger over my lips and pushed him down to the ground at my side.

If she found us here, we'd have to fight. Any chance we had of following her or learning who she'd been working for would be lost.

Aerden's body pressed close to mine on the ground, and we waited, listening for any sound of the hunter as she passed by.

Sarra Cannon

Into Darkness

Jackson

I paced the floor of the bedroom, stepping out into the hallway every few minutes just to make sure Harper wasn't back.

Yes, we needed someone here to keep an eye on the communication stones and to guard the house, but I hated the thought of them alone in that house. As far as we knew, Winterhaven had been deserted since Priestess Winter died. Her two oldest daughters, Honora and Selene, were locked in the dungeons in Harper's castle, and Zara, her youngest, was living here with us.

No one else should have had access to that house, but we had no idea what Priestess Winter's sisters could and couldn't do. It was possible they had been using Winterhaven for themselves all these months without us knowing. Zara had only been back a few times to get some of her clothes and things.

We had no idea who might be living there or using that house now.

I prayed they were safe.

They'd been gone at least an hour now, but it felt more like days to me. With the world locked in darkness, time was passing in a strange way, anyway, like an endless night where you couldn't sleep and every tick of the clock was torturous. Except no clocks were ticking tonight. Everything was silent.

Courtney was still in the guest room with Sophie, but she said she wasn't having much luck restoring the girl's power. I had tried to heal her wounds, but nothing I could do would take away the strange scratches on her skin. It was almost like they had been permanently put there.

I felt helpless.

I didn't know where my brother and Lea were or if they were having any luck in the Shadow World. So much of my group was out doing what they could to help, and I was stuck here in Brighton Manor, pacing the floors.

Footsteps in the hallway made my blood pump faster. I rushed around the corner, but no one was there.

I knocked on Courtney's door to see if she had gone into her own room to rest, but there was no answer. I went to the guest room next and opened the door slowly, not wanting to disturb them.

The bed was empty and at first, I thought maybe both of them had gone downstairs or something.

But then I saw a pale hand stretching out across the hardwoods on the other side of the bed. I ran around to find Courtney struggling for breath, trying to claw her way across the floor. I lifted her into my arms.

I placed my hand on her chest, sending my magic through her body to try to find whatever was choking her, but there was nothing physically wrong with her. She had been struck down by an evil spell, its darkness pushing back at me.

"No," I shouted. "Come on, Courtney, hang in there."

My eyes watered, and I looked toward the door, searching for Sophie. Had she been taken, too? Had whoever attacked the emerald gates come back for her?

I didn't see any sign of the girl, so I focused all of my energy on Courtney. Her eyes were wide and frightened and she reached up to grab my shirt, holding on, desperate for air.

I placed both of my hands on her chest, closing my eyes to picture her lungs. I imagined them filling with air, breathing in and out to give her life. I sent a wave of healing magic through her body, but again the darkness pushed back, locking me out.

Frantic, I reached in my pocket and found Angela's communication stone. I waved my hand over it and as soon as I heard her voice, I told her to come.

"What's happened?" she asked. "Is Harper okay?"

"It's Courtney," I said. "She can't breathe. I don't know what else to do. I need you. Hurry."

"I'm already on my way," she said.

I dropped the stone and lay Courtney down on the floor, preparing to give CPR. If magic wouldn't work, maybe I could force air into her lungs the old-fashioned way.

I tilted her head back and placed my mouth over hers, pushing my breath into her body, but the air would not pass through. I couldn't feel any kind of physical blockage, but whatever dark magic had been cast on her, it wouldn't allow any air into her body.

I leaned down, my face close to hers, trying to feel any tiny breath, but there was nothing. Her body began to seize against the floor and I put my hands on her again, trying harder to release the spell.

Angela wasn't going to make it in time.

I closed my eyes and pressed my fists against my forehead. Think, Jackson, think. What else could I do? I couldn't let her die right here in front of me.

My eyes snapped open. I could only think of one thing to do. I raised my palms and focused all of my energy on the freezing cold ice that gathered there. I placed my hands on her body one more time and blew out, allowing my freezing breath to coat her with a pale blue ice. If I could get her core body temperature down, I could potentially put her in a state of suspended life.

That would at least give Angela time to get here.

I continued until there was at least two inches of ice completely around her body. Her eyes were closed inside the icy cocoon, and I prayed she was still alive.

I stood and went to look for Sophie, thinking whoever had done this to Courtney must have taken her.

But as I stepped into the hallway, I understood too late what had happened.

I felt the hope drain from my body as a blast of energy rushed toward me. I fell to my knees, unable to lift my hands or shift in time to protect myself.

As my head hit the floor, flames erupted around me. The house was on fire.

I struggled to stand and fight, but iron chains locked around my wrists and everything around me faded into darkness.

They Needed Me

Harper

Zara and I headed back down the hallway toward Brighton Manor. I tried to wrap my head around all that was happening to us.

I wasn't sure how much more I could take.

All this time, I'd been afraid of what might happen once the remaining priestesses decided to get their revenge, but the reality was so much worse than anything I'd imagined.

The emerald priestess was always one step ahead of me, her plan already carefully formed. I was just a player in her game at this point. She moved me around on the chessboard, and I had yet to gain any real control.

And who was the woman in the dark cloak? What role did she play?

I'd believed she was trying to help us, but after seeing a vision of her there at Winterhaven, I didn't know what to think or how to make sense of it.

If she wanted to help, why didn't she just come to me? Why bother with dreams and visions?

I was so tired of having a million questions and no good answers.

The attack on the Southern Kingdom. Zara and her bloodline turning to hunters. The disappearance of my friends and allies at the emerald gates. The darkness, locked at specifically three a.m., the time most powerful for the Order, but us somehow saved from being locked inside the spell because we were not here.

It all fit together somehow, but I just couldn't see it.

I would never be able to forgive myself if Eloise and the other witches died. Yes, they knew what they were getting themselves into when they joined us, but they trusted me. They believed I was strong enough to keep them safe and to bring the Order to their knees.

I didn't want to let them down. How many had already been sacrificed to keep the priestess's spell going?

We reached the door to Brighton Manor, but when I placed my hand on the knob, it refused to open.

Confused, I tried again, turning the silver knob and pushing with all my strength.

But it was stuck.

"What's wrong?" Zara asked. She leaned against the wall, steadying herself.

"It won't open."

I took a deep breath, trying to calm the panic that threatened to take hold. Everything was fine. It was probably just rusty from not being used for so long.

But when I placed my hand on the knob again, the silver burned me. I cried out and pulled my hand away, shaking it to relieve the burning.

Something was wrong.

I reared back and kicked at the door. The wood was heavy and not easy to break through, but all I could think about was Jackson. He was home with Courtney and Sophie. If someone had attacked, they were in trouble and they needed me.

I kicked again, but the door wouldn't budge.

I backed away, taking a deep breath. I focused all my anger and rage and worry, taking it into my lungs as I spread my palms out at my side.

I reached back and with one great push forward, blew the door from its hinges.

Emerald flames consumed the door as it fell into the pentagram-shaped room in my attic. I grabbed Zara, lifting her into my arms. I shifted to white smoke and shadow and flew through the fiery wall, down the stairs to the main house, not caring about being burned. All I cared about was getting Zara to safety and finding Jackson and making sure he and the girls were alive.

I set her on the front porch and told her to run.

"Jackson," I shouted as I reformed and flew back up the stairs. I searched the rooms, but I couldn't find him through the smoke and fire that consumed my house. I ran to the guest room and screamed.

Courtney lay on the floor, her body encased in a thick sheet of rapidly melting blue ice. I tried to pick her up, but she was too heavy.

I used my mind, instead, pushing past the fatigue to lift her up.

I smashed the window with my elbow, coughing from the dark green smoke that filled the room. Flames burned my feet and my legs, but I kept my mind focused, knowing that if I concentrated on the pain, we would both be dead in minutes.

With all that I had left, I floated Courtney through the window toward the garden behind the house. I set her down near the stone fountain, and then, as the fire took hold of the entire room, shifted to smoke and flew down after her.

I knelt at her side, looking up as the only place I'd ever truly called home burned to the ground.

Sarra Cannon

Against The Darkness

Lea

The hunter made her way up a narrow path between the rocks.

Aerden and I shifted, using our powers for the first time so that we wouldn't be seen. Right now, following the hunter was the only thing that mattered. We would do what we could to cover our tracks and get far away from any sign of our magic later.

We stayed a safe distance behind her, careful not to lose her in the dark. She was using a lantern to guide her way, its light a pure amber glow against the darkness.

That magic was what I had sensed. If she had not been casting this light, she might have passed right by us unseen.

I couldn't believe our luck.

For almost two hours, we followed her up the mountain's twisting path. Finally, she stopped outside the mouth of a large cave carved into the rock on the western side. She looked around and then went inside.

Aerden and I waited a few minutes before we followed her, just in case she was watching the cave's entrance. We stuck to our demon forms, slinking through the shadows behind her.

The cave was deep, going at least half a mile into the heart of the mountain. There were several paths to take, but luckily the hunter was still using her magical light. We followed her easily, stopping when we finally saw her place the lantern on the floor and take a stone from her pocket.

We shifted back to solid form and hid behind a craggy stone that jutted out from the side of the rock.

The hunter moved her arms in a circular motion in front of her body, her robes waving like a flag. Slowly, a portal began to open over the stone she'd placed on the floor, a black hole of a thing that swirled and moved. I squinted, but couldn't make out anything on the other side of that portal. All I could see was black air, dense like a cloud.

A voice came from the void.

"You survived," the voice said.

"Yes, Priestess," the hunter answered. "The attack was a success, but we were too late. The two Winter girls in the dungeons had already changed. But there is another. The youngest, Zara. There's still time."

"How dare you call your attack a success. This whole thing should have been over by now," the priestess said. "If you had not attacked the domed city early, Harper and Zara both would have been frozen in time with the rest of the world. You almost ruined everything."

The hunter dipped her head. "I'm sorry, My Priestess," she said. "We attacked when you told us to begin. I don't understand."

"I never gave the order to attack," the priestess said. "You fools. I had everything planned to perfection. Every minor detail accounted for. You attacked two hours early."

The hunter shook her head violently. "No. We heard your voice," she said. "We heard you urging us from the shadows. We did as we were told."

"Never mind it now. It can't be changed," the priestess said. "I've had to improvise, but I can keep the world locked in time for days if I have to. I've sent my beloved daughter into the enemy's camp. She'll take care of them for me. She's attacking Brighton Manor as we speak. As soon as she captures the demon, Harper will do everything it takes to get him back. She'll walk right into our trap and never see it coming."

Aerden's hand gripped my arm. My body pulsed with fear. Brighton Manor was being attacked and she was going to capture Jackson. This whole thing had been some kind of trap.

Had we made a huge mistake leaving them there?

It took everything I had not to betray our position and run for the cave's entrance. But right now, the only advantage we had was that the hunter and her priestess didn't know we'd overheard their conversation. They didn't know we knew about the trap.

If we could just make it back to Harper and the others, maybe we could still help them defeat her.

Quietly, Aerden and I shifted and made our way back to the cave's entrance. By the time we emerged from the cave, I could hardly breathe. Sweat covered my body, and all I wanted to do was shift and fly back to the portal in the Southern Kingdom as fast as possible.

I opened my mouth to speak, but Aerden placed a fingertip on my lips to hush me. He pointed back toward the cave and I nodded, my body electric with impatience.

We shifted and flew down the mountain, not bothering with the path and taking a more direct route, skimming the surface of the stones.

We took solid form at the bottom of the mountain, and I doubled over, feeling ill.

"They'll have warning, right? There are barriers over the estate," I said. "Maybe we can still get there in time."

Aerden shook his head and ran a hand through his long, dark hair.

"The witch said the attack had already started," he said. "They're going to take Jackson, and use that to draw Harper into some kind of trap."

"We have to get back there to warn her," I said. "We have to help rescue him."

I thought I was ready to move on from my life with the Demon Liberation Movement, but knowing what they were going through proved that I still cared about them all too much to turn my back on them.

I desperately wanted to let go of the pain Jackson had caused me, but no matter what he'd chosen, I still loved him. I couldn't abandon him to the Order. We had to go back.

I started toward our camp, but stopped as the glint of steel reflected the moon's light back at me.

Aerden and I stopped as a dozen soldiers formed a circle around us.

I turned, studying the group of guards, my eyes locked on the insignia emblazoned on their chest.

A phoenix.

My father's insignia.

You Have To Let Her Go

Harper

Brighton Manor burned while I held Courtney's body in my arms. The ice had melted from around her, and I could barely feel a pulse.

Jackson must have been with her. That was the only explanation for the ice, but where was he now? I couldn't handle the thought that he might be in there somewhere, burning, with no way to help him.

Who could have done this? Getting through our defenses would have taken time. An army of witches, just like those who had attacked the domed city. There would have been some evidence of an army. Some warning. They couldn't have just vanished into thin air.

Beyond the flames, someone called my name.

I turned to see my sister, Angela, running from the woods, her eyes wide as she scanned the destruction.

"I'm here," I said. "Quickly! I don't think she's breathing."

Angela knelt at my side and pulled Courtney from my arms. She pressed the girl's damp, cold body against her own and closed her eyes. A white light pulsed from her hands as she poured her healing into Courtney, but when she opened her eyes, I could see the truth before she even spoke.

"No," I shouted, tears stinging my eyes. "Keep trying. She can't be gone."

Angela laid Courtney's body out on the grass, wiping the tears from her cheeks. "I'm sorry, Harper, she's already gone."

I threw myself over my friend's body, clinging to her. This couldn't be happening. She couldn't be dead.

"Courtney," I shouted, lifting her and shaking her, begging her to open her eyes and tell us she was okay. "Wake up. You have to wake up."

Angela put her hand on my arm. "Harper, I'm so sorry. There's nothing else I can do for her. You have to let her go."

I looked into my sister's eyes, wanting some kind of explanation. This was my friend we were talking about. Courtney was one of the innocents. She'd never done anything wrong in her life. She didn't deserve this.

I gripped her shoulders and fell across her chest, my tears falling onto her, mingling with the melted ice that covered her poor body.

I cried until I felt sick, my body shivering violently from the cold. Zara placed a hand on my shoulder.

I was going to lose them all.

"How could this happen?" I asked. "How could I let this happen?"

"It's not your fault," Angela said. She looked up at the house, eyes wide. "Where's Jackson?"

"I don't know. I couldn't find him inside," I said. "Angela, if he's in there—"

"He called me on the communication stones just a few minutes ago," she said. "He told me Courtney had been hurt and that I needed to come right away. He must have been with her."

I shook my head and stared back at the house. "I have to go back in and look for him," I said.

But as I tried to stand, Angela yanked me back down to the ground.

"It's too dangerous," Angela said. "The whole house is on fire, Harper. You'd never survive it."

"He's not inside," a voice said from behind us.

We both turned to see the girl standing near the gardenias. Sophie. Her body shivered as she walked toward us.

I stood. "What happened?" I asked. "Is Jackson okay? Did you see him?"

"He was taken," she said, tears running down her cheeks. "I couldn't see anything, but I heard them. They came into my room and brought me out here to the garden. They hurt Courtney when she tried to stop them. I think they used some kind of spell to block her breathing."

"Who?" I said. "The emerald priestess?"

"She left another message," she said. She held her hand out to me and another green stone appeared.

Trembling, I took the emerald from her hand. The moment the cool surface of it touched my skin, the dark vision of the emerald priestess appeared in my mind again. I fell to my knees, my eyes closing against my will.

"I told you I would take away everyone and everything you hold dear to your heart, young Harper," she said, smiling. "Now, I'm tired of playing games. It's time for you to act. If you ever want to see your demon alive again, you will meet me at Winterhaven. Bring Zara and my sister's ring. You have three hours."

The vision faded and I collapsed onto the ground, my strength gone. The emerald fell from my hand into the dirt, and my eyes closed, the emerald priestess's voice the only thing I could hear.

My eyes opened, and I sat straight up. I was in my bed in the domed city and suddenly all the pieces of the puzzle fell into place.

Angela was by my side, her hand on mine. Her eyes opened when I sat up, and she pulled me into her arms.

"Harper, thank God you're okay," she said. "What happened? What did that stone do to you?"

"How long have I been sleeping?" I asked, frantic.

"Half an hour," she said.

I sighed with relief and touched a hand to my aching forehead.

"There was another message in the stone," I said. "From the emerald priestess. Where is the girl? Sophie?"

"She's with Tuli," she said. "Why?"

"I want guards placed on her right away," I said. "I don't think she is who she says she is, Angela."

She shook her head. "What do you mean? She's just a girl. I thought you rescued her yourself from another sapphire gate?"

"I don't have time to explain. You just have to trust me," I said. "Tell the guards I want them to protect her. I don't want her to know I suspect her in this."

"I'll tell them," she said. She left the room for a moment, and then came back. "Harper, you have to tell me what the message said."

"The emerald priestess wants me to meet her at Winterhaven," I said. "She told me to bring two things. The ring I took from her sister's hunter, and Zara."

"Zara? But why—"

"I've been wrong this whole time," I said, feeling so stupid for not putting it together sooner. "Since this whole thing started, I thought the emerald priestess wanted revenge."

I shook my head and touched the sapphire ring I wore on my left hand.

"She doesn't want revenge for her sister's death," I said, throwing the sheets off my legs and standing. "She wants what the Order always wants. More power."

Angela moved to stand next to me.

"I'm not following you."

"She doesn't want to destroy me," I said. "She wants to reopen the sapphire gates."

How To Save Everyone

Harper

"It all makes sense," I said. "I knew the hunters who attacked the dome wanted something inside the castle, but other than weapons or jewels, I couldn't think of anything so important to bring down the whole city."

"They wanted Priestess Winter's daughters," Angela said. "From the dungeons."

"Yes," I said. "That's why none of the hunters who attacked were wearing talismans from their priestess. They were all women in Priestess Winter's bloodline. They must have been slowly turning to hunters ever since the day she was killed. That's why the emerald priestess started all this now. She's running out of time."

"But why would she need one of the Winter girls to open the gates?" Angela asked. "Why not just use one of her own witches? Or better yet, bind control of the gates to herself?"

"Because the gates are already bound to the Winter family," I said. "When the Crow Witch tried to change the family line of the Peachville gate, they killed my mother, believing she was the last of our family. With her blood, in the moment of her death, they could transfer the line from my family to theirs. Only, they didn't know about me. I was born in secret and sent to an orphanage before they killed my mother, and the spell didn't work."

"So in order for the emerald priestess to take control of the sapphire gates, they would have to kill the last of the Winter family line."

"Yes," I said. "And they would need to do it before Priestess Winter's spell took hold, turning the youngest of the family into hunters. Which is why they attacked the dome in the first place. I think they were after Honora and Selene, hoping to use them, only it was too late. They had already become hunters. I think that's why the last hunter smiled when she saw Zara. The spell had already started to take her, but she was still alive."

"But for how much longer?"

"Hours, maybe a day at most," I said, sadness so heavy in my heart, I could hardly breathe. "That's why she attacked Brighton Manor. She's getting desperate. Taking Jackson was just her way of pushing me to the limits and forcing me to give Zara up."

"We can't do that," Angela said.

"No, I won't—"

"Yes, you have to," a small voice said from the doorway.

We both turned to see Zara leaning against the stone arch of my doorway. My heart burned in my chest. Seeing her like this was devastating. Her hair was completely black now, brittle and dull. Her eyes had lost their beautiful blue shine and had turned to a milky gray. Her pale skin had dark veins snaking through it and she'd lost so much weight, she looked skeletal.

I crossed to her and helped her walk to the chair.

"I won't do it," I said. "We'll find another way to save Jackson and the others, even if we have to call in the Resistance or some other army. I won't give you up."

"You don't have a choice," she said. She placed her hand on mine and met my gaze. "I'm dying anyway. At least let me know my life ended with some greater purpose and meaning. Let me save them, Harper. I'd rather die than turn into one of those things. I can feel it happening. I can feel my humanity slipping away."

I stroked her hair and she leaned into my hand, closing her eyes.

My heart ached. Courtney was gone and now they were going to take my sweet Zara from me, too.

"It isn't fair." Angela shook her head and went to stand near the balcony that overlooked the gardens.

I paced the floor with its beautiful gemstones inlaid in the tiles, a gift from my father for a daughter he wasn't sure he would ever truly know. I wished he was here with me now, and that he could tell me how to save everyone.

But there was no one who would give me the answers. If Jackson and my friends were going to be saved, I had to make the decisions. Being a leader meant making the tough choices and letting go of those you love to save the rest. I couldn't sit around anymore, wishing things were different or that life wasn't so hard.

I'd been resisting this all along, thinking I wasn't ready, or I wasn't good enough.

But that was bullshit. The only thing holding me back was me.

It was time to stand up and be the leader my father knew I could be.

It was time for me to show the emerald priestess what happened to a witch when she messed with my family.

"I have a plan," I said.

Angela turned, her eyes wide. "What do we do?"

"We bring everyone home," I said. "And we finish this."

Sarra Cannon

The King Of The North

Lea

My father's guards placed iron shackles around our hands and feet and escorted us back to the King's City. The grand gates had been sealed shut, but there was a side passage that led directly to the castle. The guards brought us through this secret passage and led us to the throne room.

The King of the North sat on a golden throne, his shoulders slumped and his head slightly ducked and leaning to one side.

As angry as I was to be brought back to my own home in chains, the rage did not compare to the agony that gripped me when I saw him. He barely looked like himself. His hair had grown long and wild, and his eyes were a dark red color, greatly changed from their normal amber glow.

When he saw me, there was only the briefest flash of sympathy and love before he narrowed his eyes and tightened his grip on his scepter.

The guards threw us to the ground at the bottom of the steps leading to the throne. The chains clattered against the alabaster floor, the sound echoing off the walls and ceiling.

Aerden and I bowed our heads and waited for him to speak.

Footsteps sounded on the floor as someone ran out from a nearby room. "Lazalea," my mother said, her voice already rattled with sobs.

My father looked to her, anger and warning in his eyes. She stopped, glancing from him to me, her hands outstretched. She straightened her shoulders and went to stand beside her husband, the king. She placed a hand on the back of the throne and kept her eyes facing downward, but I could tell she was crying.

I hadn't seen my mother in more than thirty years, and being brought in like a common criminal was not exactly how I saw my return going down. I longed to go to her and feel her warm arms surround me. I wanted more than anything to hear my parents say they had made a terrible mistake.

For years, they told me trying to rescue Aerden was a fool's task, and yet here he was, kneeling at my side, free.

Something told me they hadn't brought us here to apologize.

"Stand," my father said.

Aerden and I stood side by side, his arm brushing mine, as if to let me know we were in this together.

"You are both brought here on the charge of treason," the king said. "What say you to this charge?"

I met his gaze, looking for any resemblance to the great demon I had admired as a shadowling. His body and spirit were still strong, but his mind was leaving him.

What has happened to you, Father?

I wanted to ask more than anything, but I knew he wouldn't be able to answer me. The mad don't know they are descending into madness. Something had changed him, though, more than I ever expected. In only thirty years, how had he deteriorated so much?

"We have committed no treason," I answered. "I'm begging you to set us free so that we can go back to the human world and warn our friends that a great battle is coming. A great betrayal. Please, Father, I'm asking as your daughter, to let us go."

"You are no daughter of mine. You directly disobeyed the order of your king," he shouted, slamming his scepter into the arm of his throne. "I warned you not to interfere with the business of the

Order of Shadows. I told you not to meddle with the dealings in the human world. I told you to leave that boy to his fate. You betrayed me."

"How can saving someone we all care about be considered a betrayal?" I asked, standing straight and tall. "If anyone has committed treason in this room, it's you, Father. You've turned your back on your own people, leaving them unprotected. What has become of you?"

"You will not speak to me in this manner, child, or I will have you thrown in the dungeons."

"Throw me in your dungeons if you must," I said. "But I will not admit to treason. The only wrong I have done is believing in you. You were once a great demon. A great king. Now, you abandon all hope and hide yourself inside these city walls while the rest of your kingdom fights for their very survival. It is you who should be brought to trial. Not me."

"Daughter, don't," my mother cried out. "You'll only make it worse."

"Speaking the truth shouldn't be a crime, Mother," I said. "If you had only admitted the truth when Aerden was first taken, we might have saved him sooner. But you lied to me and to Denaer."

I used the name given to Jackson at birth, Denaer, since my parents didn't know him by his human name. But even then, my pleading did nothing to stir their sympathy. I could see it in my father's eyes. He wasn't going to let us go.

"You turned your back on Aerden, telling me that he was as good as dead. Well, here he is," I said, turning to him. "He's safe and alive and free. I was a part of that, Father. It's not too late to join the fight against the Order. Those who helped Denaer and me save his brother are still out there fighting, and they are in danger. Let us go now, and you can be a part of saving thousands and returning them to their lives here in the Northern Kingdom."

"Your lies are of no use here, girl," my father said, standing. "Guards, throw them into the dungeons until we can have an official trial with the Council."

"What treason has Aerden committed, my king? He has done nothing against you. He has disobeyed no orders from you," I said. "What reason do you have for throwing him in the dungeons?"

"He abandoned his duty to the Royal Guard when he left the city a hundred years ago," he said. "Guards!"

They seized us, taking us by the arms. I struggled against them, kicking and trying to shift, but the chains had been enchanted to take away my ability to transform.

"You're making a mistake," I shouted. "Denaer and Harper are in danger. They're the only ones left who can save our world from the Order. You have to at least let me get a message to them."

But my father and mother had already turned away, their backs facing me as they walked to the king's chambers on the other side of the room. They disappeared inside, not listening to my screams of protest.

The guards marched us out of the throne room and down a dark hallway. When they reached a spiral stone staircase on the far side of the castle, they forced us down floor after floor, deep into the ground, and shut us inside adjoining cells with enchanted iron bars.

I shouted at the guards to let me go, but none of them paid any attention. They didn't care that I was a princess and that my father had obviously lost his mind. They blindly followed the orders of their king, leaving us in semi-darkness half a mile below ground.

I kicked and slammed my hands against the bars, cursing.

How could he live with himself, throwing his own daughter into the dark dungeons he reserved for criminals? All I'd ever wanted to do was be loyal to the demon I loved. I'd followed him, wanting to free his brother, my dear friend.

Somehow, throughout the years, his war had become my war.

I wanted to see an end to the Order of Shadows just as much, if not more, than he did. Not solely because of what had happened to Aerden, but because over time, I realized just how many of my own people had been taken and forced into slavery.

And now, the only friends who had ever worked alongside me to face the Order were in trouble, and I was helpless to warn them.

I kicked the bars again and Aerden laughed.

I turned to look at him. "How can you possibly laugh at a time like this?"

He shrugged and leaned against the bars. "You have no idea how ridiculous you look, kicking at those bars with a plain leather boot, as if they will suddenly give way and allow you to escape."

I rolled my eyes and turned away from him. "Now is not the time to be laughing. Our friends and family are in danger, and we're stuck in here with no way to help them or warn them. There's nothing funny about that."

"No, it isn't funny," he said. "But kicking the bars is not going to get us out of here."

"What will?"

"Well, accusing the king of treason is probably not the first step." He raised an eyebrow, and I couldn't help but smile, despite the dungeon around us.

I sighed and leaned against the stone wall. At least they had placed us in adjoining cells. It could have been worse.

"When you live in captivity for a very long time, you learn to either accept your fate and resign yourself to hopelessness, or you find a way to hope," he said, his hand on the bars between us.

"Which did you do?" I asked.

He leaned against his fist and thought for a moment. "I chose despair and hopelessness," he said. "Especially after I saw Jackson come through and get bound to human form, his magic stripped away. Immortality sucks when you have nothing to live for. I don't want to be that way anymore."

His eyes met mine and I swallowed, my mouth suddenly dry.

"Why did you leave?" I asked softly. "On our engagement day?"

Aerden didn't take his eyes off mine for a long time. "I just had to go," he said.

It wasn't much of an answer, but I knew it was the only one I would get for now. I slid down the wall and rested my arms on my knees. How were we going to get out of here?

What would be left of our group when we finally did?

I think in that moment I understood a little of what made Harper such a bleeding heart. She loved her friends more than life, and she cared more about what happened to us than what happened to her. It was easy to forget how young she was sometimes. She carried the responsibility of two worlds on her shoulders.

I probably should have cut her some slack.

"They're going to be okay," Aerden said, crouching down to my level. "They're strong. And Harper's smarter than you give her credit for. No matter how much it hurts or how unfair it is, she loves my brother. She'll give everything to save him, you know that. We have to believe, Lea, or there will be nothing left to fight for."

"I just wish we were there," I said. I cut my eyes toward him and half-smiled. "Besides, I would have loved to kick a little more Order ass."

He laughed and leaned back against the bars. We sat that way for a long time, not saying a word.

I wanted to believe him. They would be fine.

But if that was true, why did I already feel such a strong sense of loss?

Risk Everything

Harper

I activated all of the communication stones, asking everyone to get to the castle as soon as possible. I asked Mary Anne and Essex to bring Rend. Even if he didn't have a potion that could save Zara from turning into a hunter, he might still be able to help us.

Mordecai, Joost, Cristo, and Erick got there quickly, using their demon speed to travel in the dark of the endless night on earth. Mary Anne and the others arrived less than an hour later, traveling by demon door to Cypress and then flying the rest of the way.

When Rend appeared in the throne room, he had ten large men with him, their ruby eyes startling me at first.

"Vampires?" I asked, almost breathless. Vampire demons drank the blood of witches to gain power, and seeing them in my father's castle was a shock, to say the least.

"Good vampires," Rend said with a smile. "Mostly, anyway. They're friends, and they know you helped us when we needed you. They'll be loyal. Plus, I promised them they could finish off any of the witches on the evil side during the fight."

I let my eyes wander over the eleven of them, my heart beating wildly. They were handsome and rugged and extremely powerful. Every witch's worst nightmare. But I trusted Rend with my life and knew he would never do anything to hurt us.

Franki, his girlfriend, hugged me and promised she would do everything she could to help. A few more of their friends from Rend's club, Venom, also joined us to fight. Azure, the bartender, and Marco, another of Rend's close friends.

"Thank you for coming," I said. "This isn't going to be an easy fight."

"Good," a tall, muscular vampire said. "I wouldn't want it any other way."

"Calm down, Ryken, you'll get your chance," Rend said, patting his friend on the arm.

As I shared my plan with them, Gregory came through the doors and announced that the Resistance had arrived. I let out a sigh of relief, feeling some of the tension and worry in my shoulders give way.

Andros walked through the door and bowed at my feet. "Princess."

I held my hand to him and helped him up. "I wasn't sure you'd come," I said. "I know I'm not your favorite person in the world."

"You are a true warrior, and while I don't always agree with your methods, I agree with your cause," he said. "If this is truly another opportunity to put an end to one of the priestesses of the Order of Shadows, I will lay down my life, and the life of every one of my soldiers to get it done. I only wish Lea were here."

"I couldn't reach her on her communication stone," I said. "She and Aerden are out searching for a hunter who attacked us a few days ago."

"I'm sure they can handle themselves," he said. "But their abilities would be useful in this fight. I'm sure they will be sad they weren't here to see the end of the emerald priestess."

"I'm sure," I said with a smile.

His beautiful pixie of a wife, Ourelia, came forward and bowed her head. I pulled her into a hug. "Thanks, Ourelia," I said. "I know it's difficult to leave your daughter behind, but I promise my guards here in the castle will make her safety a priority."

Their small shadowling daughter, Sasha, rushed forward and clung to her mother's legs. I turned around and searched for my sister, and when our eyes met, I nodded to her. Ryder, a young boy Jackson and I had rescued from the Northern Kingdom months ago when we traveled to the south from the Underground, ran forward and took Sasha's hand. Together, they followed Tuli to an area of the castle reserved for special guests. She had set up a room just for them where they could play games and have plenty of food and things to do.

"Now that everyone's here, I'd like to go through my plan," I said.

I outlined the basics, making sure everyone understood when to make their move. "Rend, do you think you can use the laboratory here to make these potions?" I asked. "I know I'm not giving you much time."

"I'll get to work on it right away," he said. "I may have to pull some things from your gardens."

"Anything you need," I said.

He and Franki disappeared to go work on the three main potions I needed to make my plan work. The rest of us gathered weapons and dressed for battle.

An hour later, when everything was in place, I found Zara and pulled her to me. Her body was so frail and weak, it stunned me. She'd been full of life and joy just a few short days ago, and now her mother's evil was reaching out from the grave to take her away from us.

"Are you sure you're up for this?" I asked.

She nodded, tears in her eyes.

"I love you, you know that," I said, wanting to hold her tighter, but so scared I might hurt her. "Thank you for doing this. You have been a true friend since the day we met. You've given up everything you knew and loved to do what was right, and it's not fair that this is happening to you. I swear I will not let you die in vain."

We held each other for a long time, tears running down our cheeks.

"I've asked Andros to send for a powerful shaman who lives in the Underground," I said. "Maybe she can help."

"Harper," Rend said softly.

I pulled away and wiped at my cheeks. "Do you have them?" I asked.

He nodded and handed me three small vials. The moment my hand touched them, my stomach tightened into knots. It was time.

"We're almost ready," I said. "I just need to do one more thing."

I met Angela's eyes and nodded. She whispered something to the guards and they all took off down the hallway.

I took Zara's hand in mine and helped her walk with me to my father's chambers. Angela, Sophie, and the guards joined us soon after.

I held one of the potions out to Zara. "Drink this," I said. "It will at least allow you to walk in there with some dignity."

She nodded and drank the potion down quickly.

I handed out the other two potions and watched as they disappeared. I prayed my plan would save us all. Lea always accused me of taking unnecessary risks, and I had doubted myself every step of the way lately. But tonight, there was no playing it safe.

It was either lose everything I loved and allow the priestess to undo everything I'd worked to achieve, or risk everything for a chance at victory.

"We're ready," Angela said.

"I'll catch up with you in a second."

Angela escorted the others from the room, but before I joined them, I went back into my father's bedroom and stared up at the gleaming sword on the wall.

I carefully removed it from its mount and gripped the shining hilt in my hands.

"Be with me now, Father," I whispered to the sapphire stone that held a piece of his spirit.

The stone shimmered, and I felt his presence with me, making me stronger.

I'd been so scared to carry his weapon with me over the past few months, always feeling that I wasn't worthy of his sacrifice. I was terrified I would never live up to what he wanted me to be.

But as I held it in my hands, I realized for the first time that all he'd ever expected was for me to be myself.

I'd always felt like a victim of my circumstances, brought into this fight at birth without a choice in the matter. I needed to stop letting this war be something that just happened to me. I may be young, but that didn't make me weak.

I was capable of amazing things. I refused to let them beat me.

It was time to stop letting the Order call all the shots and show them how powerful you could be when you ruled with love instead of pain.

I secured the sword to a strap on my back and headed out to lead my army toward Winterhaven.

Not The Normal Way Of Things

Harper

Since Brighton Manor had burned to the ground, we had no demon door left to use in Peachville. The army I'd assembled made their way through the darkness to Cypress, one of the closest demon gates to us.

The others remained inside Eloise's house, while Zara and I walked up to the pentagram-shaped room in the attic alone.

Her body trembled as I ushered her through the Hall of Doorways, searching for the one with the blue butterfly. When we found it, she hesitated, pulling back on my arm, but she was too weak to resist.

"It'll all be over soon," I whispered.

We stepped through the door to Winterhaven, where a woman in an emerald green cloak waited for us. She smiled as we entered.

"Priestess Evers will be happy to see you."

"Let's just make the trade so I can get my friends home safely," I said.

"You'll have to leave that sword here, I'm afraid," she said.

I tensed my jaw and nodded, removing my father's sword and laying it down on the floor. I hoped someone would be smart enough to bring it down with them when they came to wreck this place.

The woman laughed and held out her hand, motioning for us to walk down the narrow stairway to the second floor. I knew exactly which route to take. I'd been here more times than I'd ever wanted to, and each one had been a source of fear and horror.

I hoped when I left here tonight, it would be with a feeling of triumph.

The stairs near the kitchen creaked as we made our way down to the basement's ritual room. I could hardly feel my hands, I was so nervous. They were numb and ice-cold. I searched the room as we entered, looking for any sign of Jackson.

"Harper, don't," he said. "You can't do this."

I turned toward his voice in the dark room and nearly wept with joy to see him alive. They had him in an iron cage in the corner. I moved toward him, but the woman in the green cloak placed her arm between us.

"You'll get to cuddle your filthy demon when you've made the trade and the portal is reopened," she said, her voice biting.

I lifted my head and straightened my shoulders. So, I was right. That's all the emerald priestess ever wanted. This wasn't about revenge. This was about her gaining more power than any of her sisters ever dreamed.

I couldn't wait to introduce that witch to my father's sword.

The ritual room was lit with dark green candles floating above our heads. At least two dozen witches in matching green cloaks surrounded the broken portal stone embedded in the floor, their hoods pulled over their heads to hide their faces.

I searched for Priestess Evers. I'd never seen her in person, but I knew her from her messages in the green stones.

She stood on the far corner of the pentagram carved into the stone floor. She wore a flowing black robe with emerald scarab beetles embroidered along the skirt. My heart jolted, remembering Sophie's pendant.

I was right.

Priestess Evers lowered her hood as we came in, and her eyes were so startlingly green that I almost lost myself in them.

She looked young, just like her sister had. Considering the witch was more than two hundred years old, she was holding up pretty well on her diet of souls.

She had blazing red hair the color of autumn leaves, and she smiled at me as I entered. She glanced at the witch beside her and nodded. The woman curtsied and came over to me, taking my hand from Zara's arm and escorting her to the center of the portal stone.

My stomach bubbled with nerves and my heart ached for what I was about to see. How had it all come to this so quickly? Just a few days ago, we were celebrating Halloween and an engagement. Everyone was happy, and Zara had looked like a sprite with her white-blonde hair and pale skin.

She was a shadow of herself now, dark and decaying, the life almost gone from her completely.

She struggled against the witch who held her as best she could, but she was too weak to resist. She stumbled as they brought her to stand on the ritual stone. Her frightened eyes pleaded with mine, and I looked away. She tried to speak, but her voice wouldn't work.

"I can't tell you how happy I am to finally meet the infamous Harper Brighton," Priestess Evers said. "I'm sure this has been a rough few days for you, Princess, so I promise I'll make this short and sweet. Trust me, this would have been a lot easier for all of us if my stupid hunters hadn't attacked your city a few hours too early."

"What do you mean?" I asked, confused.

"They weren't supposed to attack until after I'd frozen time here in the human world," she said. "You were supposed to be locked in time just like all the rest of the miserable humans on earth. I planned to just waltz into your home and put an end to you. I was going to take your ring and kill your friends and be done with it. But the hunters attacked early, sending you and your friends to the Shadow World, where my spell wouldn't affect you. It was an unintended series of events. That's why I had to improvise and take all those witches you made friends with from my emerald gates. I needed the fuel to keep my spell going for as long as it took."

"Eloise," I said. "Is she alive?"

"Yes, yes, your darling Eloise and her two daughters are still alive. I can't say the same for some of the witches in her coven, though, poor things," she said. "It's taken you so long to get here and give me what I want that twenty-six witches have had to die. That's on your head, my dear."

I shook my head and closed my eyes, praying those witches had not suffered long.

"Of course, simply casting the spell took the sacrifice of one hundred young witches," she said.

My eyes snapped open and I stared at her, not believing it.

"What?"

"Trainees who fled their duties when the sapphire gates fell," she said. "We hunted them down on Halloween and cut their throats one by one. They were expendable, really. Girls who were supposed to become members of the sapphire gate covens, but who went into hiding instead of turning themselves in to join another coven. Your old friend Allison was one we searched for, but the little darling got away from us. Pity. She's a powerful one."

I placed my hand over my mouth. Allison had been a cheerleader in the same grade as me at Peachville High. She and her mother had disappeared shortly after Priestess Winter died, and I hadn't heard from them since. Thank God she had managed to escape from the emerald priestess, but I felt sick thinking of all the girls who had died.

"So many have sacrificed so much to bring us here to this moment, and unless you want to see another of your allies sliced up to hold us through for another hour, I suggest you hand me that sapphire ring."

I slid the sapphire ring from my finger and tossed it through the air toward the priestess. It landed at her feet with a clanging sound, and she raised an eyebrow at me.

"So much fire and passion," she said. "You would have made a very good Prima, you know."

She lifted her hand and the ring rose from the ground.

In order to reopen the gates, she would have to perform the original ceremony the sisters had used to open the five gates. She needed five items to complete it. A chalice. A dagger. A necklace. A ring. And a master stone.

Four of those items now sat on a small table at Priestess Evers's side. I knew from experience that the master stone was inside her body, serving as her heart, and fueling her evil.

"We're almost ready to begin," she said. "All I need now is my daughter."

"Your daughter?" I asked, looking around the room.

"Sophie, dear, can you come inside, please?"

I turned toward the door and the young girl I thought I'd saved from the ruins of a sapphire gate came walking down the steps and into the room.

At her breast, she wore the emerald scarab pin.

My fingers went numb, and I felt like I could hardly breathe.

She smiled at me and then walked to her mother. They clasped hands.

"One thing you learn when you rule over thousands of witches for two centuries is that the most valuable commodity is trust," Priestess Evers said. "If you can get your enemy to trust someone close to you, then you can always betray them when the moment is right."

She smiled down at her daughter and cupped her face in her hand.

"You did good, sweet girl," she said. "I hope you're ready to take over your own covens as the new priestess of the sapphire gates."

"I'm ready," Sophie said.

"Then let's begin."

With a nod of her head, several cloaked witches took their spots on the other four points of the pentagram star and knelt on the stone floor. Two others wrapped their arms around me, placing chains on my wrists to keep me from shifting to my demon form. I struggled against them, but I knew it was no use.

I concentrated on the army waiting on the other side of the demon door. They were our hope and our future now. It was all in

231

their hands.

Priestess Evers began reciting the ritual words and when she stood on the fifth and final mark of the star, the sapphire portal stone healed itself, bursting forth with a shining blue light. Zara's body tilted, floating in the air lengthwise above the stone. She tried to scream, but it came out as a dull groan.

As the priestess continued the ritual, the light grew brighter and black swirling smoke crept from the opening inside the light.

Priestess Evers looked to a witch standing in the hallway that led toward the room full of cages. "Bring forth the demon."

The witch nodded and began to cast a spell.

An iron cage floated from the darkness of the hallway, a demon woman in a black cloak locked inside. I breathed in sharply. I may not have ever seen her face, but I knew this demon. She had come to me in my dreams and warned me this was coming.

They marched her toward the portal stone as everyone in the room watched, holding our breath.

This was not the normal way of things. Normally, a demon was chosen in the Shadow World and pulled through the portal. I'd never heard of a demon being brought and held captive here in the human world.

When they opened the cage and brought her to stand beside the portal stone, the witch ushering her out lowered the woman's hood and she looked at me, her face full of sadness and regret.

"No," Jackson shouted. He beat against the iron cage they held him in. "How could you? You can't do this. You can't have her."

I turned to him, not understanding at first. But then the demon looked to him and smiled, tears running down her face.

"Brother, how I have missed you," she said.

I gasped, nearly dropping to my knees. It couldn't be. How much horror could one family endure?

"Illana, no. I can't lose you, too," he said, sobbing and falling to the floor of the cage.

My eyes filled with tears. This was not part of my plan. I wasn't sure I'd be able to save her, but how could I have known?

She was the one who had tried to warn us both, all this time. I'd wondered so many times why the cloaked woman hadn't just come to us and told us what was going on, but now it all made sense.

She couldn't come to us because she was locked up, held prisoner by the emerald priestess until the ceremony could be completed.

"Quiet," Priestess Evers said. She pushed her energy toward Jackson and he raised a hand to his mouth, his eyes wide with panic. He couldn't speak.

Illana lowered her head and waited as the ceremony continued.

"Illana, demon of the Shadow World, we bind you. Enter into this holy vessel, we command you," Priestess Evers began.

Illana gasped and shifted to black shadow, her body pulled into the circle. The dark essence of her spirit swirled around Zara's body like smoke.

Priestess Evers took the necklace, the chalice, and the dagger from the table and walked to Zara's side. She grabbed her wrist and held it out as she sliced across her pale and withering skin. Blue blood poured from Zara's wrist and fell into the chalice.

"*Animus compingere moderatus,*" the witches around us chanted.

Priestess Evers dropped the necklace into the chalice of blood, a hissing sound echoing in the chamber as the blood began to bubble and boil. She handed the cup to Sophie and returned to Zara with the dagger.

Everything inside me screamed out to put a stop to this. It felt unnatural and horrible, seeing her so helpless.

I couldn't stand to watch it, but I refused to turn away. Tears fell from my eyes.

"*Adnexus ab cognatus,*" Priestess Evers called out as she placed the dagger against Zara's throat.

233

Sarra Cannon

Full Of Tears

Aerden

The dungeons of the castle were dank and dark, an unpleasant smell wafting from the sewers.

It was cold down here, and I shivered. As a natural fire caster, I was more susceptible to the cold, feeling it deep in my core.

Lea had fallen asleep, tired from kicking the bars and struggling to try to shift. She should know better than anyone how hopeless it was to think you could escape these dungeons.

But to me, even this captivity was nothing compared to what I had endured in the human world. At least here, I was left to my own thoughts, instead of constantly being drained by someone else's abuse of my power.

A door squeaked on its iron hinges as it opened, and I stood from my resting place on the floor and walked to the front of the small cell.

I peered out to see who had come, hoping maybe the king had changed his mind and agreed to at least let us warn Jackson about the betrayer. But my eyes filled with tears as the woman approaching let down her hood and revealed her face.

"Mother," I said softly.

Tears fell from her eyes and she reached for my hands through the bars. "Is it really you?" she said, her voice a whisper in the darkness. "I never thought I would see you again."

She placed her hand on my face and caressed it gently.

Something inside me opened, like a wall coming down, unable to hold back one hundred years of abandonment and agony.

"Why didn't you come for me?" I asked. My lip trembled as I spoke the words. I had just told my own brother that they should have left me behind, and I thought I believed that with all my heart. But seeing her here, feeling her skin upon mine, I realized just how angry I was that my own parents had turned their backs on me.

Jackson was the one who'd fought for me. He sacrificed everything, even his own chance to rule this kingdom, to save me. And I had treated him like shit, blaming him for Lea's sadness. I hadn't even given him the chance to explain or defend himself.

Now, he was in danger, and there was nothing I could do to help him.

"Mother, you have to get us out of here," I said. "I don't know your reasons for leaving me to the Order, but you have to understand that Denaer doesn't deserve this. He's given up everything to save me. He's engaged, Mother, to someone he truly loves. He's happy. And he might die if we don't warn him what's coming."

She pulled her hand from the bars and stepped away, turning her head to the side so I couldn't see her face.

"You and your brother don't understand how this world works," she said. "You think it's as easy as swooping in there with some army and taking out the Order of Shadows, but there is so much more you don't know."

"Then tell me," I said. "Tell me why you can't fight them. Why does the king lock himself away and abandon all of the other demons in the outer villages? I don't understand."

"Aerden, it's not our place to question the king—"

"Then whose place is it? He's gone mad, Mother. Can't you see that? I've been gone over a hundred years, and he barely looked at me. He didn't welcome me home or rejoice that one of his worst enemies had been defeated," I said, careful not to wake Lea. "Instead of rejoicing and joining the fight to help us defeat the Order, he locked everyone in this city away and abandoned the rest. Have you been outside the gates? Have you seen what's happened to the cities there? I saw it with my own eyes as the guards marched us here in chains. Places that once thrived with life are ghost towns. How is that good for any of us?"

"Oh, my sweet child, I don't know how to make you understand," she said, raising her hand as if she wanted to touch me again, but reconsidered and drew back. "I have to go before they find me here, but I had to come see you. I had to make sure you were real and not just some dream."

"I need to ask you something first," I said.

"Anything," she said.

"Has the king brought a stone guardian here to the city?" I asked it in a hushed whisper, terrified to know the answer.

The skin around her eyes twitched and she stepped forward. "Where did you hear that?"

"So it's true?"

She breathed in slowly and shook her head. "I can't discuss this with you. I need to go."

"Mother, wait," I pleaded. "If they won't let me get word to my brother, can you do it? In our bags there's a ruby communication stone that allows us to get in touch with him or with Harper. We need to warn them before it's too late. If it isn't already. Please, I'm begging you."

"I can't, Aerden. Can't you see that? I'm powerless to help, and if I was discovered communicating with the future Queen of the South, I don't know what would happen to your father and me. It's bad enough I've lost so many of my beautiful children. I can't afford to lose what we have here in the King's City, too. I have to keep Orian safe, and I have to do what I can to keep you safe now that you've returned to me."

My blood turned ice-cold. "What do you mean? Where's Illana? Mother, where's my other sister?"

237

She turned to me, her eyes again full of tears. "She's gone, Aerden," she said. "When she heard of the fall of the sapphire gates and that you had been saved, she begged the king to let us leave the city and find you. But he refused, saying that no one was allowed in or out, with threat of treason if anyone was found trying to escape the city. She stayed for a few months, but recently, she'd grown depressed and impatient. I should have recognized the signs. Paid more attention."

"What did she do?" I asked.

"She sold some of her jewels and hired two guards to escort her from the city," my mother said. "When the guards returned, they said they'd been attacked by a group of powerful hunters. They said Illana was taken. Don't you see that this is why the king has locked us away? It's for our own good, to protect us all. Once you leave this city, there's nothing I can do to help you. Illana is gone, just like your brother."

She placed her hands on the bars, looking at me with such sweetness in her eyes. I almost couldn't bear to look at her. How could she say she cared about us when she could so easily turn away?

"But you've been returned to me," she said. "And I will do everything in my power to keep you here, where you're safe. I know the dungeons aren't comfortable. I'll try to make sure they're bringing you warm food and blankets to keep you from catching cold. But thank God, you're safe, my sweet boy."

"Mother—"

"I have to go," she said, turning her head at the sound of someone approaching. She placed her hood over her face and touched my hand one last time before she ran down the corridor and disappeared into the darkness.

I walked over to the bars that separated me from Lea and slid down the length of them, reaching my hand through to touch hers as she slept. Her eyes fluttered open and she smiled at me for a moment before they closed again.

I had no idea how we were going to escape or if Jackson and the others in the human world were going to be okay, but I was used to uncertainty and fear. I'd lived with it for so long, it had broken me.

Over time, I'd given up on my own life and freedom a long time ago, never daring to dream that I would ever again be able to feel the softness of her skin or the way my heart beat when her eyes met mine.

Immortality is torture when you have nothing left to live for, but for the first time in as long as I could remember, hope blossomed inside me.

Maybe Jackson was right. Maybe it was time to tell her the truth.

I rested my head against the bars and closed my eyes, deciding that once we both woke in the morning, we'd find our way out of the darkness of this dungeon and head toward the light we'd both left behind so many years ago.

Sarra Cannon

The Sorrow For All I'd Lost

Harper

Death comes to us all, eventually. But there is nothing more devastating than watching someone you loved die right in front of you.

The silver blade of the dagger sliced across Zara's throat, and blood poured from her like a wave of tears.

My body rigid, I breathed in as her life flowed outward, puddling on the surface of the sapphire portal stone. The emerald priestess smiled and waited, ready to pass the power of the demon gate to her daughter. I watched the excitement and ecstasy in her eyes, forcing myself to see the kind of evil I was fighting against.

Whenever I doubted myself in the future, and whenever the battle seemed too hard, too costly, I would remember that look in her eyes. Anyone who could find such joy in the death of a soul so pure and innocent as Zara's deserved to burn in hell.

And tonight, that's exactly where I planned to send her.

The last of the blood drained from Zara's body and she fell, lifeless, to the floor. The dark shadow of the demon swirling around her slowed and hovered like a cloud above her.

The priestess's smile faltered and she wiped the dagger's blood on her robes. She tugged at her hair and glanced at her daughter. I waited and watched, biting the inside of my lip.

She motioned for Sophie to join her, her neck stiff and her movements jerky.

"*Daemon Ingredieris huc,*" she said, her voice echoing in the still room.

Nothing happened.

Priestess Evers stared at the Shadow Demon, her eyes widening, anger flashing like lightning.

The bright blue light of the portal stone began to fade and the demon started to shift, her human form appearing in the smoke.

The priestess shook her head in quick, pulsing movements back and forth.

She ran a trembling hand across her forehead. "I don't understand," she said, her voice hoarse and grating. "Something's not right."

Her emerald eyes narrowed and she looked from Zara's body to the chalice, trying to make sense of what was happening.

My stomach rolled in waves of nervous anticipation.

Finally, she snapped her head toward me. "What have you done?" she asked.

It was my turn to smile. I raised an eyebrow and tilted my head. "I wanted you to be surprised," I said.

I turned to Sophie and in a loud, confident voice, said the words that released the power of Rend's glamour potions.

"*Exero.*"

The body lying dead across the portal stone changed as the glamour dropped. Blood covered Sophie's neck and hair, her eyes lifeless and unseeing.

Rend had created three potions. Zara's potion gave her strength and glamoured her to look like Sophie.

Sophie's did the opposite, making her look like Zara.

The third potion had taken Sophie's voice away so she wouldn't be able to scream or protest or tell anyone I had switched their appearances.

The potions didn't take any concentration to maintain and could be dropped with that one word. *Exero.*

Zara's eyes met mine and tears coated my lashes. I might not be able to save her from her mother's curse, but I would never willingly let her die by another's hand.

"Go," I mouthed.

I wanted her out of there before the priestess and her coven had a chance to wrap their minds around what had just happened.

Zara nodded and shifted into a small blue butterfly. She disappeared into the hallway and up the stairs.

The silver ritual dagger clattered against the stone as it dropped from the priestess's hand. She stared at the lifeless body of her most cherished daughter.

Her arms shook and her mouth opened. Her face twisted in rage and misery as the horror of what I'd done soaked into her evil brain. She dropped to the stone floor and screamed, her hands reaching up to tear at her fiery red hair.

Crawling, she clawed at Sophie's body, pulling the girl into her arms and violently rocking her back and forth. Sobs choked her as she wailed, blood soaking her robes.

The room erupted in chaos. Some witches ran to console their priestess, while others turned their eyes to me.

The footsteps of an entire army pounded on the narrow staircase leading down from the kitchen. Rend and his vampires came first, their shadowed forms flying across the room in every direction, descending on witches of the Order and sinking their ivory fangs into flesh.

The witch who had ushered us downstairs earlier grabbed the ritual dagger from the floor and rushed toward me with wild eyes, screaming.

Black smoke coiled around her feet and she dropped to the floor, her head landing on the stone with an awful thud. Blood gushed from her, spreading out through the cracks in the floor like a maze of gore. I searched for the source of the smoke and met eyes with Jackson's sister, Illana. She nodded slowly, pulling smoky tendrils of power back toward her body.

She shifted easily and reappeared next to me. Her hands closed around the iron shackles at my wrists and they popped open.

"Thank you," I said.

She touched my wrist, and though she didn't speak, everything she wanted to say was there in her eyes.

She shifted again and flew toward the cage that held Jackson hostage.

I ran to help and just as I reached them, Andros called my name. I turned and he held up my father's sword, admiration in his dark eyes. I wrapped my hands around its hilt, grateful for its weight and power.

Jackson climbed out of the cage and pulled his sister tightly to his body. His eyes met mine, grateful tears shimmering in the light of the spells that clashed and erupted throughout the room.

"Find Eloise," I told him. "She's here somewhere. I can feel her."

He nodded and both he and Illana shifted and flew down the dark hallway toward the room of cages.

I turned and searched through the chaos for the emerald priestess. She wasn't near the portal stone, and her daughter's body was gone, too. I shifted and snaked through the bodies toward where I'd last seen her. I followed the trail of blood up the stairs, through the kitchen, and up to the second floor.

How had she escaped through all the fighting? Had no one seen her leave?

She must have cloaked herself in some kind of invisibility, so I moved carefully, my sword held out, mentally preparing to shift or attack if necessary.

My feet crisscrossed on the grand staircase, every sense on high alert.

The trail of blood stopped at the top of the stairs, and I turned in a circle, searching for any sign of where she went. I was sure she was heading for the Hall of Doorways to make her escape, but as I approached the secret entrance to the attic, a scream tore through the hall behind me.

I shifted and turned, flying backward, a bolt of lightning barely missing me. Green flames erupted next to me, and I drew back my sword, aiming for her heart. If I had to, I would carve the master stone out of her chest.

Priestess Evers disappeared, and I stopped just short of the grand staircase, spinning around. Where had she gone?

I stepped forward carefully, listening for any sound of breath or movement. I passed the secret entrance to the attic again, but just as I took the next step, I felt a whisper of air brush across my left arm.

I swung the sword out to the left and the priestess fell to her knees as the edge of the blade sliced through her side.

She lowered her chin and lifted her eyes to me, pure rage burning inside.

"You murdered my beloved daughter," she said.

"No, you did that," I said.

I rushed forward, sword first, but she was faster than I expected. She raised her right fist and threw something at me. I raised my hands to shield my eyes as shards of green jewels sliced into my skin from head to toe. Pain ripped through me, and my sword fell to the ground.

I struggled to shift to my demon form, but the pain held onto me, dulling my concentration. I stumbled and blinked several times, my vision blurring.

For a moment, everything seemed to move in slow motion. A green light glowed in Priestess Evers's hands and she sent the force of it toward me. I tried to raise my arms, but just like when I'd been poisoned in the domed city, I felt like I could barely move my hands. Had the shards of glass poisoned me?

Something pushed against my arm and before I realized what was happening, Zara screamed and jumped in front of me. She must have come up here to hide in her old bedroom until the fighting was over.

The burst of green lightning crashed into her chest. She jerked and fell to the floor, a blackened gash across most of the front of her body.

"Harper," she said, terror blossoming in her eyes. Every inch of her grew rigid and then released, the light in her eyes dimming as her head fell to the side.

A low, guttural sound vibrated my chest. My hands tightened into angry fists, my shoulders shaking uncontrollably. Overwhelming pain pulsed through the cuts in my skin, but all I could think about was my friend lying dead in front of me.

Thunder rumbled and raindrops fell into my hair and down my cheeks. Wind howled through the hallway, blowing my hair across my face.

I blinked again, trying desperately to clear my vision, but even with limited sight, I could see the priestess preparing her next attack.

I shifted to smoke just as she cast her next bolt of lightning and reappeared behind her. Before she had time to turn, I pushed my sword straight through her spine.

She made a strange gurgling sound as green blood bubbled from her mouth and poured from her chest. I lifted my foot to her back and pushed her body forward. My sword slid from the wound with a sucking sound, and she fell face-down on the floor.

The sorrow for all I'd lost at the hands of this woman flooded through me, rain falling in sheets across my skin.

I knelt beside the priestess and put my hands under her body, lifting hard to flip her over. Her eyes were open and she gasped for air. I aimed for her heart, the tip of the blade pushing straight through to the floor. With a sawing motion, I cut a jagged line down the left side of her chest where her heart should be.

The priestess moaned and tried to stand. I raised my palm in the air and then pressed downward with my magic, forcing her back to the ground.

I dropped my sword and dug my fingers into her bleeding chest, reaching through the cracks of the wound and searching for the slick, bloody surface of the emerald master stone.

Beneath me, the priestess laughed and then coughed, green blood dripping from the side of her mouth. "You won't find it," she said, raising her hand to wipe the blood from her cheek. "Do you really think I'd be dumb enough to bring the master stone with me?"

A wave of dizziness crashed over me and I shook my head, trying to focus. Whoozy, I lurched forward, leaning one hand against the floor near the priestess's head to steady myself.

"You surprised me, I'll give you that," she said, coughing again. "Not many people surprise me. But I also knew you were strong and had an army willing to fight at your side. Just in case things went wrong, I left my heart at home. You can do whatever you want to my body. Burn me, cut me into pieces, stab me through the chest a thousand times. None of it will kill me as long as I still maintain a connection to that stone."

"How?" I asked. I raised a hand to my forehead, feeling ill. I struggled to stay upright, my skin suddenly feverish and sweaty.

"That's one secret you'll have to discover on your own," she said. "My sister may have been older, but she was not smarter. Too bad that's something you had to learn the hard way."

I sat up, dark green blood coating my hands. I took several deep breaths, trying to steady my heart. What was happening to me? The rain had stopped, and a voice deep inside told me to run. Find help. But when I tried to stand, my legs gave out and I dropped hard against the floor.

I turned over and clawed at the shards of green stone stuck in my skin. I pulled a few out, but when I reached for the next one, my fingers suddenly stopped working. I couldn't force enough strength in my grip to pull the shard out of my flesh. My fingers simply slipped off the surface over and over.

Priestess Evers sat up. She looked like hell, maimed and bleeding, but she was smiling, her lips stretched over her teeth as she leaned her head back and laughed.

"I bet you thought you had me, didn't you?" she asked. She clucked her tongue three times, shaking her head. "You should know better than to think you could kill a second priestess so easily. Nothing went as planned for me, but maybe this will work out better."

She stood and put one foot on either side of my hips. The expression on her face as she looked down at me chilled me to the bone. I began to cry, praying that someone would come looking for me. I should never have followed her up here alone.

"You're so incredibly powerful," she said, bending her knees and crouching just above my legs. "You're going to be a great addition to my collection."

"Collection?" I asked, my voice a ghost of itself, barely more than a whisper.

She simply laughed again and pushed her bloodied hair back from her face, leaving a streak of green across her forehead.

"Don't worry, Harper, this won't last much longer," she said. "Soon, you'll forget all of it. Your friends. Your dead father. Your precious demon boyfriend. Everything. And then you'll be mine to fill with whatever lies I choose. I can't wait to mold you into the perfect new daughter."

I whimpered, tears cascading down my temples and into my hair. "Jackson," I whispered.

The priestess leaned forward and wrapped her fingers around my necklace. She yanked hard, the chain pressing into the flesh at the back of my neck before it snapped and released.

She stared at the golden locket and the blue sapphire pendant I kept together on my chain. Almost reverently, she ran her thumb across the top of the gemstone. "You won't be needing these anymore," she said.

I closed my eyes, heartbreaking agony flowing through me like acid, and tried to connect to my power. If I could just shift one last time, I could make it down the stairs to where the others were fighting.

But it was no use.

Whatever poison ran through my veins had dulled any sense of power within me. I opened my eyes for a moment, watching as the priestess threw my necklace against the wall. She stood and moved around behind me, lifting my arms at the wrist.

She dragged me across the floor, past Zara's body and up the stairs toward the Hall of Doorways.

My eyelids closed for the last time, all the fight gone from my body.

I won't forget you, I whispered to myself as sleep pulled me deep into a pit of darkness.

Sarra Cannon

Wrath

Jackson

The last of the witches surrendered, falling to her knees at my feet. I grabbed her by the wrists and lifted her, pushing her toward the others. Mordecai and Joost stood guard over them, ten in all. The rest were dead.

"We did it," I said to Andros, gripping his forearm.

"What about the emerald priestess?" he asked. "Did she escape?"

I looked around the room, unsure of what had happened to her. "She disappeared during the fight. I was hoping maybe someone in the Resistance or one of the vampires from Rend's group had gone after her."

Andros cursed and ran a hand through his long, black hair. "None of my soldiers have seen her," he said. "And Rend's vampires are all here."

I put my hand on his shoulders. "The important thing is that we stopped the ritual and were able to save the witches from the emerald gates who'd been taken prisoner," I said. "We'll kill the emerald priestess another time."

He nodded, his jaw tense. "Did you find Eloise and the others?"

I nodded. "The priestess had created a magical dungeon here in the basement to hold them all. They were here the whole time, but no one could see them unless they knew where to look. Eloise is talking to them now. As soon as we get things settled out here and have made sure the emerald priestess is really gone, we'll start leading them home through the Hall of Doorways."

"The spell is broken," Mary Anne said, running up to us. She smiled and took in a huge breath, letting it out as she slumped forward in relief. Essex put his arm around her shoulder, his face beaming. "The clocks in the house have all started up again. It's over. The emerald priestess must be either dead or long gone."

"Where's Harper?" I asked, stretching my neck to search through the crowded ritual room. I'd lost her in the chaos of the fight. With so many people packed into one small room, it had been impossible to tell what was going on there for a while.

I couldn't wait to pull her into my arms and take her home to the castle. All I wanted to do for the next week was hold her captive in our bed while our bodies and souls healed from the events of the past few days.

There would be a lot of rebuilding to do. Brighton Manor was gone, and the dome around the castle would need to be restored to its full power, but that would all come in time. For now, the battle was over and everyone was safe.

My heart soared. Harper had been amazing. When Sophie betrayed us and brought down Brighton Manor, it had felt like the end of the world. I knew Harper would come for me, but I had no idea how she would be able to save Zara's life or prevent the ritual from happening.

The dark hours I'd spent alone in that cage, waiting for the ritual to begin, were the longest of my life.

But when she'd entered the room with Zara and Sophie, I'd realized all over again just how brilliant she could be.

I could see through glamours, but that was a rare gift. The priestess hadn't known what she was doing when she'd slit the throat of her own daughter. It was a risky move on Harper's part, but she'd somehow managed to save us all.

Where was she?

"Excuse me," I said to Andros, pushing through the crowd.

252

My sister Illana placed a hand on my arm, and I stopped. I hugged her close, hardly able to believe she was really here with me now.

"You were the one showing me those visions?" I asked. "And Harper's dreams? I didn't know you could do that."

"I wanted to come here to find you," she said. "When I'd discovered the truth about Aerden being set free after all this time, I begged Mother to convince the king to let us leave the city and search for you. I wanted to bring you home to us."

"He let you go?" I asked.

She shook her head, glancing toward the floor. "No. He refused. I kept trying to convince them, but after a while, I grew impatient to see you. It's been too long, my brother," she said, throwing her arms around me again. "I missed you both so much. I hired guards to escort me through a secret tunnel that led beyond the wall. I'd planned to go to the castle in the Southern Kingdom to look for you. The rumors were that you'd joined an alliance with the future Queen of the South, so I knew if I could find her, I would find you as well. But we were ambushed by a group of hunters before we'd even reached the borderlands. The guards fled, and I was captured."

"I'm so sorry, Illana," I said. "We didn't know, or we would have come for you sooner."

"That's why I tried to reach out to you," she said. "I couldn't come to you directly, but my powers of telepathy have become stronger over time. I reached out to you first, trying to warn you of their plans, but no matter how hard I tried, I couldn't show you my true self. My powers were weakened inside the cage. So through you, I tried to reach inside Harper's mind, but it was too difficult."

"I'm just glad you're safe now," I said.

"Where's Aerden?" She glanced around the room. "I'm dying to see him."

"He and Lea went to the Northern Kingdom to track down one of the hunters who attacked the castle in the south," I said. "We haven't been able to reach them."

Worry wrinkled her face. "Do you think they're alright?"

"I'm sure they're fine," I said.

I didn't want to scare her, but I was worried about them, too. They should have at least checked in by now. They were both strong warriors, but even the strongest could be taken down in battle. If they didn't contact us in the next day or two, maybe Harper and I would go looking for them.

I searched the room again, waiting for her deep brown eyes to meet mine. I was anxious to hold her in my arms and feel her lips against mine. We'd been through hell, but we were finally beginning to see the light.

"Have you seen Harper?" I asked as Angela passed by.

She shook her head, her eyes darkening. "You can't find her?"

Worry knotted in my stomach. "I haven't seen her," I said. "Maybe she went to find Zara. My magic couldn't remove the curse, but Andros called for his mystic as soon as he heard what was happening. She should be here by now. Maybe they're all together."

Zara had looked so frail and dark, her body deteriorating quickly. I wasn't sure what they'd been able to find out about a cure, but it made sense that Harper would have gone to look for her. Zara had run up the stairs after the glamours dropped, so I quickly pushed my way through the crowd of vampire demons standing near the staircase.

I made my way through the first floor and up the grand staircase, but as soon as I stepped into the second-floor hallway, my heart stopped beating.

What the hell had happened up here?

Blood and water coated the hardwood floors. A woman in a long, flowing dress, her hair braided with beads, crouched above the body of my friend. I recognized her from our time in the Underground. She was a friend of Andros and Ourelia's, and was trained as a mystical shaman.

I walked to her, my heart breaking as I stared down at the wound across Zara's chest.

"What happened here?" I asked, kneeling beside them.

The shaman priestess shook her head. "I'm not sure," she said. "I got here as quickly as I could, but this is exactly how I found her, poor child."

"Is she dead?"

The shaman reached into a worn leather bag at her side and took out a small bottle of purple liquid. She uncorked the top and closed her eyes, moving the bottle in a circle above Zara's wound. Soft words flowed from her lips and she brought her hands back to her own chest, holding them in a prayer position as the bottle floated in the air.

I'd seen her perform a similar ritual when she'd healed Mary Anne several months ago in the Shadow World. I waited, praying she would be able to help Zara, too.

Steam rose from the potion, and the priestess leaned forward, cupping her hands and wafting the smoke toward her in a repeating pattern. Her eyes opened, their blue color changed to a dimly glowing lilac.

She began to sing, the notes low in her chest. With her left hand, she gripped the potion and turned the bottle upside down, the steaming liquid falling toward Zara's body.

I held my breath, watching and praying for any kind of reaction. A scream. A twitch. Anything to prove Zara was still alive.

But she didn't move at all. Her body lay still and lifeless, her delicate beauty marred by the darkness that had taken over in the past few days. I closed my eyes, a tear falling down my cheek as I reached out to take Zara's hand in mine.

It wasn't fair. Had the emerald priestess done this to her?

Movement nudged against my hand, and I sat up, startled.

I backed away as silvery threads sprouted like thin vines from her chest. They stretched out toward her feet and head, wrapping around her until she was completely encased in them. I swiped a hand across my face to clear the tears from my eyes.

What was happening?

I looked at the shaman for answers. A peaceful smile had settled on her face. "I don't understand," I said.

"She's a butterfly, yes?"

I nodded, my breath hitching in my chest, my lungs refusing to open.

"Her body has entered a cocoon." The shaman gently lowered her ear to Zara's body. "She's resting, preparing for a great transformation."

"You mean, she's alive?"

"Yes," she said, her eyes returning to their natural deep blue as she placed the empty bottle in her bag.

"What about the curse?" I asked.

"Sometimes even the darkest magic cannot dim the light of the purest souls," she said, resting her hand on the cocoon and closing her eyes. When she opened them again, she nodded, as if understanding something she hadn't a moment before. "This witch sacrificed herself for someone out of love, and her selflessness broke the curse."

Sacrificed?

My heart clenched, and I swallowed, glancing at the horror scene around us.

Something lying on the floor near the wall caught my eye, and my world shattered. I couldn't breathe. It was like someone had reached inside me and torn my heart out.

I stood and crossed to the necklace, praying I wasn't seeing clearly. It couldn't be hers. It just couldn't.

I crouched down and struggled against the panic that threatened to overcome me.

Harper's necklace lay in a pool of blood, the chain snapped and broken. I closed my eyes as I took a deep breath, my chest tightening.

The mystic placed a hand on my shoulder. "What is it?" she asked. "Are you okay?"

I shook my head, unable to answer. I couldn't speak. I couldn't even think.

I reached down and clasped the locket in my hand, holding it up to my heart.

Where was she? Was she still alive?

I spun on the balls of my feet and searched the hallway, my eyes seeking any clues as to what happened here.

I touched my hand to the streaks of blood that ran along the floors. Green mixed with red. My body broke out in a terrible fever as I rubbed the green blood between my fingertips.

The emerald priestess.

She must have fled up the steps toward the Hall of Doorways. Had Harper followed her?

Two green shards of glass lay in the middle of the floor, but when I reached for them, the shaman grabbed my arm and shook her head.

"I wouldn't touch those, if I were you," she said, her eyes wide. "They're poisoned with dark magic."

My hand trembled as I wiped blood across the leg of my jeans.

Harper had been poisoned.

This couldn't be happening again. I'd already lost my brother to the Order, and it had taken me a hundred years to save him. I couldn't bear going through that again. Not with her.

I couldn't live without her.

My eyes followed the smear of blood that led from where I'd found the necklace to the entrance of the hidden staircase leading up to the attic. I shifted and flew up toward the pentagram-shaped room at the top. The blood led straight to the Hall of Doorways.

Breathless, I flung the demon door open and followed as far as I could, shifting back to my human form when the trail of blood thinned and disappeared.

I stared at the door to my right, an emerald scarab beetle carved in glowing green on its surface. There was no doorknob, and when I pushed and pounded on the door, the magic locked inside burned my skin. There was no way inside.

I cried out and fell to my knees, my heart shattering into a million pieces.

Why? Why had she gone after the priestess alone?

Why hadn't I looked for her sooner? I should have sought her out, made sure she was safe.

I pressed my fists to my forehead, my body trembling and hot with fear.

Sobs rocked my shoulders as I doubled over, the pain of losing her so great, I wasn't sure how I'd be able to survive it.

I will find you, I thought, hoping that somehow, wherever she was now, whatever she was going through, she would be able to sense my presence. My undying love.

I promise, even if it takes the rest of my immortal life, I'll never rest until you're safe in my arms again.

Exhausted and broken, I struggled to my feet and stared at the door, every muscle in my body rigid as rage took hold.

I'd been called Wrath once because, in my anger and sorrow, I'd forced my way into this world through blood and death to try to save my brother.

Dark shadows swirled around me as the fury of a long-lost fire ignited within my soul.

Clutching the golden locket in my fist, I vowed that this time, it wouldn't take a hundred years. This time, I would teach them all the true meaning of the word wrath.

Emerald Darkness

About the Author

Sarra Cannon writes contemporary and paranormal fiction with both teen and college aged characters. Her novels often stem from her own experiences growing up in the small town of Hawkinsville, Georgia, where she learned that being popular always comes at a price and relationships are rarely as simple as they seem.

Her best selling Young Adult paranormal series, Peachville High Demons, has sold over 200,000 copies, and has spawned an entire world of different series, including Sacrifice Me and the new continuation series starting with Emerald Darkness.

She is a devoted (obsessed) fan of Hello Kitty and has an extensive collection that decorates her desk as she writes. She currently lives in South Carolina with her amazingly supportive husband and her adorable son.

Connect with Sarra online!
Website: SarraCannon.com
Facebook: Facebook.com/sarracannon
Instagram: instagram.com/sarracannon
Twitter: twitter.com/sarramaria
Goodreads: Goodreads.com/Sarra_Cannon